D0108902

This book has been
DISCARDED
from the library.

Deliver Us From Normal

KATE KLISE

DELIVER US FROM
~~Welcome to~~
NORMAL

SCHOLASTIC
PRESS

NEW YORK

Library of Congress Cataloging-in-Publication Data

Klise, Kate.

Deliver us from Normal / by Kate Klise.—1st ed.

p. cm.

Summary: With a mother who buys Christmas cards in August and
a younger brother who describes the Trinity as a toasted marshmallow
on a graham cracker, life for eleven-year-old Charles Harrisong is anything but normal in Normal, Illinois.

ISBN 0-439-52322-2 (alk. paper)

[1. Family life—Illinois—Fiction. 2. Family life—Alabama—Fiction.
3. Interpersonal relations—Fiction. 4. Self-perception—Fiction.
5. Catholic Church—Fiction. 6. Schools—Fiction. 7. Moving,
Household—Fiction.] I. Title.

PZ7.K684De2005   [Fic]—dc22

2004042906

10 9 8 7 6 5 4 3 2   05 06 07 08 09

The text was set in Adobe Garamond

Book design by Elizabeth B. Parisi

Printed in the U.S.A.   23

First edition, March 2005

For my sister Sarah, of course

He jerked his head at Dill: "Things haven't caught up with that one's instinct yet. Let him get a little older and he won't get sick and cry. Maybe things'll strike him as being — not quite right, say, but he won't cry, not when he gets a few years on him."

— Harper Lee, *To Kill a Mockingbird*

Nothing mattered but getting away.

— Marjorie Kinnan Rawlings, *The Yearling*

BOOK ONE

Prologue

I grew up in a mustard yellow brick house in Normal, Illinois.

Yes, there really *is* a Normal, Illinois. I should know. I was born there.

There's also a Peculiar, Missouri. We drove through Peculiar on our way to Kansas City. That was the summer I turned eleven.

We had our picture taken in front of a sign: WELCOME TO PECULIAR, WHERE THE ODDS ARE WITH YOU! My mom wanted to use the photo for our Christmas card that year. And, since it was cheaper to buy photo Christmas cards in the summer, she ordered them at the annual Christmas-in-August sale at Bargain Bonanza.

But we never sent them. We left the cards behind when we left our yellow brick house in Normal in the middle of the night.

Years later I realized they were red bricks painted mustard yellow. As a child, I thought yellow bricks were a different kind of brick, just like ours was a different kind of family.

1.

My name is Charles Harrisong. I'm the oldest boy and the second-oldest child in the Harrisong family. *(Welcome to the Harrisongs, Where the ODDS Are with You!)* My sister Clara is a year older than me. Ben's three years younger. Laura's two years younger than Ben. And Sally's the baby.

Other than summer vacations and Boy Scout camp, which I attended for the first (and last) time in July of that same Peculiar summer, my family rarely left Normal. I always thought we'd live in Normal forever. Or at least until I finished sixth grade.

Clara's election changed all that.

Which is not to say that my sister was elected president of her seventh-grade class. It's funny. Until just this moment I'd always assumed Clara lost — and by a significant margin. It amuses me now to think that maybe she won the election; that maybe we left Normal for no reason.

No, there was a reason. Let me see if I can explain. Well, first let me see if I can remember.

Start at Bargain Bonanza, the huge discount shopping center designed to look like a dude ranch. It was the last store inside the city limits of Normal.

When you pulled through the gates of Bargain Bonanza (YER DADGUM DISCOUNT LEADER!), if you were like me, you'd try to avoid eye contact with the waving rodeo clowns standing under the HOWDY, PARDNERS! sign.

So you'd look to your left (if you were coming from town) and see the green sign next to the highway: THANKS FOR VISITING NORMAL!

Years ago some high school kids spray-painted the word BEING in black letters over VISITING. So the sign read: THANKS FOR BEING NORMAL! No one ever replaced the sign or removed the graffiti.

I grew up thinking that was our city motto: *Thanks for BEING Normal!* It was a polite way of expressing our town's only commandment: *BE Normal!* They made it sound so easy.

For my family, *being* normal wasn't easy. Looking back, I don't know if it was even possible.

Okay, so don't start at Bargain Bonanza. Start with our house. Look at the rooms inside the house. Study the people in those rooms. What did they say? What did they do? What decisions did they make, often late at night, with a staggering lack (in retrospect) of reliable information.

How did they possibly think any of it would work out?

Start in August, when it all began.

*   *   *

It was the week before school started, and summer was putting up its last brave little attempt to fight off fall. But of course a lazy late summer was no match for the inevitable autumn with its stern back-to-school lists issued by the Normal Public School System.

When the school supply lists arrived in Monday afternoon's mail, my mom taped them to the refrigerator, over the park district summer pool schedule and a laminated Prayer of St. Francis.

I was eleven years old and pleasantly surprised to see that my list, *Required School Supplies for ALL Normal P.S. Sixth Graders,* did not include a single offensive item. Not one of those maddeningly childish things from elementary school, like crayons or glue sticks. Instead, my list (*My First Ever Junior High School Supply list!*) was short and no-nonsense: 6 wide-ruled notebooks, 10 pens (blue or black ink), 10 pencils with erasers, 500 sheets loose-leaf paper, wide-rule. I memorized the list easily with something that felt like maturity.

My brother, Ben, was eight. He took one look at the third-grade list and covered it with action figure stickers — dozens of them — until the list was unreadable. Mom didn't notice it until she was making dinner. When she did, she told Ben he would have to arrange to get a new school supply list, even if it meant calling school. Even if it meant talking to a teacher. *Or* the principal.

"Dumb old school," Ben said, pulling a half-used Hot Wheels notebook out of the junk drawer in the pantry. He had a purple action figure sticker the size of a half-dollar stuck to the center of his forehead.

An hour later, I was back at the refrigerator, reading my list again to make sure it hadn't changed. Ben was stretched out in a corner of the kitchen floor, talking on the phone. He was allegedly getting his list from a friend, but in fact he was roaring with laughter. He had to put the phone down occasionally to cover his eyes and howl. The list he'd started *(NotBooks Sizzers Pencell Powch)* was ripped in two pieces, the smaller of which was stuck by static cling to his curly brown hair.

My mother was standing at the stove, stirring butterscotch pudding and watching Ben. I knew Mom knew she would have to get Ben's school supply list for him — just as she knew she would never have to get a list for me. It might seem like a small difference, but it's something every child and every parent knows: Some kids are good at making and remembering lists. Some kids aren't.

Back then, I was a list keeper. Ben wasn't. God only knows what Clara was.

2.

The morning after the school supply lists arrived, we made our annual pilgrimage to Bargain Bonanza for back-to-school shopping.

Clara was twelve and looking forward to starting seventh grade at Normal Junior High.

"A lot of girls in my class carry purses instead of backpacks," Clara told Mom as we pulled into Hitchin' Post Section C of the Bargain Bonanza parking lot. "Do you think I should get a purse? I mean, it seems sorta silly, right?"

"I need a purse!" said Laura, who was starting first grade at Normal Elementary. "That's what I *really* wanted for my birthday: a purse."

Laura turned six in July and had spent the weeks since her birthday remembering all the things she *really* wanted: a deck of magic cards, stilts, a trophy, a *real* doll factory.

"Now just a minute," Mom began, turning off the ignition. "We're shopping for school supplies, shoes, and —"

Sally interrupted her: "I needa burse, too!"

Sally was four years old and didn't go to school yet.

"Where's *my* burse?" Sally asked, arms outstretched.

"I don't want no stinkin' *purse,*" said Ben, sliding out of the car. "Now a *horse* would be good. But not a purse. No *way* a purse!"

Ben had recently become obsessed with all things Western. I blamed Bargain Bonanza in part for this. I also blamed the discount giant for stocking the school supply lists for every grade, K through 12, at the main entrance to the store. Because, as it turned out, I was the one who had to get Ben's list. A half hour before we'd left for Bargain Bonanza, Mom asked me to ride my bike over to the elementary school office to pick up a copy of Ben's school supply list. I did without complaint. (Both the elementary and junior high schools were only blocks from our house.) But now I saw the trip was a waste of time, as did Ben.

"Hey, Mom!" Ben yelled, pulling a handful of lists from the shelf labeled THIRD-GRADE SCHOOL SUPPLIES. "Here's that dang list you wanted."

"Mom," Laura said. "If I have to pick just one, a horse or a purse, I think I'd like a horse. Please."

"I needa burse *AND* a horse," Sally announced. "A burse and a horse! A burse and a horse!"

"Quiet down," Mom said, pulling from her purse a shopping list written on one of Laura's abandoned connect-the-dot drawings. "No one's getting a horse. I'll think about purses."

She selected a shopping cart from the herd of abandoned carts in the Cart Corral (*Head 'Em Up! Move 'Em Out!*) at the front of the store. The cart she picked had a front right wheel that made an odd, croaking noise — *ERK, ERK, ERK* — every time it rotated.

"Now," Mom said, struggling with the errant cart, "there's one thing I know you all need."

"Ice cream!" said Laura.

"Horses!" said Ben.

"Underwear," corrected Mom, looking squarely at Ben. "Especially *you,* young man. I saw a pair of your underwear in the laundry this morning. It had a hole in it as big as an I-don't-know-what and —"

"I don't have HOLES in my UNDERWEAR!" hollered Ben.

We were only to the SHAKE OFF THE DUST AND LET'S SHOP! sign. But already, dozens of shoppers were looking up from the cheap clothes that hung limply from ropes tied to wooden posts. The shoppers smiled, elbowed one another, and stared in our direction.

I saw the stares not with my eyes, which I had trained to stay focused on the clownishly oversized boot prints painted on the Bargain Bonanza floor, but with my skin. My pores absorbed those staring eyes like a new kitchen sponge absorbs water.

This, I believed, was my secret gift: I could see and hear things — words, messages, hidden meanings — without my eyes and ears. I could feel things other people didn't feel. At times it made me feel strangely holy in a *Blessed-are-they-who-did-not-see-and-yet-believed* kind of way. But mainly I felt strange. My family didn't exactly help.

"Ben has holes in his underwear, Ben has holes in his underwear," Laura sang, waving her arms over her head like a lawn sprinkler — left, right, left, right — and flinging her hips in the opposite direction.

"Well, you've got holes in your *brain!*" Ben countered.

"I'd rather have holes in my brain than holes in my underwear!" Laura yelled.

"Only a person with holes in her brain would say *that,* you big knucklehead!" Ben said. And he laughed triumphantly at his inspired comeback.

"Ben called me a *bucklehead!*"

"*Bucklehead?!*" Ben said. "I said *knucklehead.* You can't even say *knucklehead!*"

Laura stomped her foot twice and then burst into tears. We were almost at the stage of creating an official scene. We were ahead of schedule.

By habit, I recited my silent prayer: *Please God, don't let me see anyone I know. Please God, don't let me see anyone I know. Please God, don't let me see anyone I know.*

"Mom, can I go to the bakery department and watch the cake decorators?" asked Clara.

"Not until we pick out new underwear," Mom said. "We'll look at cakes after we look at underwear and shoes and school supplies. And then maybe —"

"Hey!" Sally hollered. "I needa horse and a burse in my umberwear!"

And that's how we walked down Cowpoke Avenue, the main aisle of Bargain Bonanza: talking about cakes, horses, *burses,* and holes in underwear while trying to keep our cart from running into the hay bales.

To appreciate Bargain Bonanza, you should know that enormous round hay bales were scattered throughout the store. You should also know that the Bargain Bonanza jingle ("Roundin' up bargains, drivin' down prices, woo hoo woo hoo, it's all for YOU!") was my favorite song until I was ten and knew better.

Somebody in upper management must have thought hay bales were a cheap way of adding atmosphere to a 750,000-square-foot discount store. I imagined a bunch of rich men in suits sitting around a conference table at the Bargain

Bonanza headquarters in Dallas, laughing about this brilliant hay-bales-as-décor scam.

"What about plastic cow patties, too?" a top executive might ask his colleagues. "All over the floor. You know, give Bargain Bonanza a real authentic ranch look!"

Cow patties! The bloated executives would explode in laughter.

"But why *plastic?*" another suit would say. "Why not real ones? Everything in those stores is *crap,* anyway!"

HaHaHaHaHaHaHaHaHaHaHaHa!

These were the conversations that played in my head whenever we shopped at Bargain Bonanza. The truth was, I didn't hate the people responsible for the hay bales. I was grateful for that hay. It was my cover. I spent much of my youth at Bargain Bonanza, my back pinned to one of those huge hay bales, praying I wouldn't see anybody I —

"Hey, it's Charlie Harrisong!"

"Hi, Charlie!"

"Howdy, Charlie!"

Courtney, Michelle, and Taylor. The three most popular girls in my fifth-grade class.

"We're shopping for purses!" Taylor said brightly. "Wanna shop with us?"

The three most popular girls giggled. It was a laughter

that I knew said something other than good-natured humor. Using my secret gift, I decoded the message behind the laughter: "Look at us! We're popular girls, but we're talking to Charlie Harrisong — *Charlie Harrisong!* — like he's a *normal* kid. When everyone *knooooooooows* Charlie Harrisong is *sooooooo* not *normal.*"

"He *can't* shop for purses!" said Laura, wiping her shoulder against her tear-drenched face. "Charles has to shop for —"

"Notebooks!" I said. "Notebooks!"

My voice didn't even sound like me. I sounded like a puppet.

"Notebooks," I repeated. "For school. Notebooks!"

Why was I speaking in this strange puppet voice? Why was I repeating myself?

A cardboard cutout of Cowboy Cal, the fictional founder of Bargain Bonanza, twirled from the ceiling, directly over my head.

"Just . . . notebooks," I said again. And then I turned and bolted down the nearest aisle, Dude Drive. I took a quick right and hid among the Tupperware containers and plastic storage bins on Stuff Fer Storin' Yer Stuff Road.

But even there I could hear Clara singing along with the Bargain Bonanza jingle, now adapted for the season. The song was streaming from the beige speakers mounted clumsily throughout the store.

"Roundin' up bargains is always COOL! Woo hoo woo hoo! It's back to SCHOOL!"

My older sister sang the last line like an opera singer. ("It's baaaaaack tooooooooo schoooooool!") I could hear her giggling at her alter-ego cartoonish self.

But Clara's gentle laugh was drowned out by the chorus of popular girls cackling. Their gaudy, lip-glossed choir swirled with the sound of my family parading down Cowpoke Avenue and the mocking squeal of our shopping cart: *ERK, ERK, ERK.*

So much for prayers. So much for *BEING* normal.

3.

I can't explain why the sound of a broken shopping cart wheel had the power to humiliate me. It just did. A lot of things did.

Our last name: Harrisong. The fact that everyone misspelled it: *Harrison, Harrissong, Haresong.*

Our family car: a ten-year-old powder blue station wagon. My dad's truck.

My dad didn't embarrass me. He was okay. It was just his rattletrap truck *("Charles, come help me hang the ladder on the truck, will you?")* and especially the graphic painted on the back of the truck next to: FRANK HARRISONG: A NORMAL GUY WHO DOES ODD JOBS. I often wondered why my father, a man who could fix anything, would choose for his logo an overall-clad buffoon with a squiggly line for a mouth, looking with crossed eyes at a winking hammer in one hand and a swollen, tomato red thumb in the other.

My mom worked from home, sewing slipcovers for furniture. She had no truck and no business logo. I sometimes thanked God for this, just as a preventive measure on the off chance Mom was considering getting a truck or a logo.

We'd taken our summer vacation to Kansas City so Mom could show her sewing to a woman named Babette, who owned a chain of fancy little shops called Bow-tique. I could tell the meeting with Babette didn't go well.

"Some people are just *born* on the wrong side of the bed," Mom had said with a shudder when she climbed back into the station wagon. Her slipcover and pillow sham samples were wadded up and tucked protectively under her arm. Then, looking at Dad: "I *told* you this'd never work."

Other things that embarrassed me:

Our mustard yellow brick house. The spooky-looking bushes in front.

My teeth. Specifically, the ridges along the bottom.

My freckles. Specifically, the monster ones on my arms.

My clothes. Specifically, the Bargain Bonanza–brand dress shirts my mom picked out for me. (At least she didn't make me wear the matching neckerchiefs that came with them.)

The Harrisong hair, which is best described by the fact that, for Halloween one year, all five kids washed our hair and let it air-dry without combing it. We went as tumbleweeds. Without being told, several people guessed what we were.

The way my sister Clara called me Chums or Chumsley. Ben's Ben-ness.

The fact that Laura cried about everything (and often in public).

The fact that Sally called me *Barley* until she was three.

The rodeo clowns at the entrance to Bargain Bonanza. I wasn't embarrassed by them. I was embarrassed *for* them. Grown men — and a lot of them were *old* — dressed like clowns, waving to kids? It made me sad to think of them driving home at night and seeing creepy old clown faces in their rearview mirrors, and then realizing those faces were theirs.

*   *   *

After much discussion, Clara decided on a royal blue plastic tackle box instead of a purse. (*"Look at all these funny little compartments!"*) Laura got a Hello Kitty backpack and a coin purse shaped like a cat. Ben got a leather pouch to tie around his belt loop.

"This is how *real* cowboys carry their lunch money," Ben told Mom as we stood at the photo counter picking up our Christmas cards. (*Christmas cards. In August.*)

Sally got rabbit stickers. I got notebooks. I also got in trouble for waiting outside Bargain Bonanza under the HAPPY TRAILS! sign while Mom was still inside, paying for our purchases. But it was worth it. The thought of those popular girls seeing my family *and* our Christmas cards *and* our underwear . . . it was unthinkable.

"You know, Charles, everyone wears underwear," Dad told me that night, when he came to say good night to Ben and me in the bedroom we shared.

Ben giggled under the covers in his bed across the room.

"'Member that time in first grade I *forgot?*" Ben said to the wall. I could hear his bed shaking with laughter.

"Ben, please," said Dad. "I'm trying to talk to Charles."

"Can we just *not* talk about it?" I asked. "Please?"

"I understand," Dad said.

And I knew he didn't understand. He was just trying to be nice. Still. Why couldn't we be a normal family? The fact that we lived in Normal and *weren't* only compounded the problem. Maybe we should move to Peculiar. Maybe we'd fit in there.

That night, like most nights, Mom came in after Dad. She had the library book she'd been reading to Ben and me for the past week: *World's Great Explorers, Volume 2*. She sat on Ben's bed and began reading to us about the men with the magical names: Magellan, Balboa, Ponce de León.

When she read, my mom alternated beds. She read exactly ten pages on Ben's bed and ten pages on mine. When she sat on my bed, Mom used her index finger to tickle the hair on my head in big circles. It felt so good. Sometimes I even lost count of my pages.

Ben usually fell asleep before Mom finished reading. His snoring, strangely regular and constant, provided the white noise soundtrack of my childhood. I listened to it for years, waiting to fall asleep, creating the lists that lived in my head: *Things to Worry About. Questions I Wish I Could Ask Someone Really Smart. Ways My Body Is Weird: a) The Too Much* list *b) The Not Enough* list. *The Most Embarrassing Things in My Life* list.

I reviewed my lists every night. It was my falling asleep ritual. But somehow with time the lists grew longer, forcing me to add new categories and sub-lists, until my falling asleep ritual began keeping me awake for hours.

So I began alternating my lists with a prayer. For years I said the same prayer every night and again at church on Sundays: *God, please let us be a normal family. Let us get a normal car. Let us live in a normal house and do normal things and not always be so embarrassing and different and loud. This is all I want. Please. Thank You. Amen.*

Some nights I added a P.S. to my prayer: *Give me a sign if You can hear me, God. Just a little sign. Just for me.*

4.

At dinner on the Friday before school started, Ben was explaining his main grievance about school.

"See, they give you homework, but they never give you home*play*," Ben began, licking a spoonful of lime Jell-O. "So you have to *work* at school and *work* at home and nobody ever lets you *play*."

"More hash browns, anyone?" Mom asked.

"Right here, please," Dad said.

Ben's spoon and chin sank to the table as he released a theatrical sigh. His argument was being ignored.

"Well, *I* got to play at *my* school," Laura offered.

"But that wasn't *real* school," Ben said, exasperated. "That was *kindergarten*. In *real* school, you never ever get to —"

"Ben," Mom said sharply. "Turn the page."

Silence. The sad sound of summer leaking out of the air.

"Then maybe I'll just go to kindergarten again," Laura said carefully, still trying to read the old page. "'Cause I liked kindergarten. I'll just stay in kindergarten. That's a good idea, right?"

Clara, who sat across the round table from Laura, leaned forward on her elbows and said, almost confidentially, "Laura, you are going to love first grade."

Clara said the words *first grade* with a reverence we usually reserved for sacred things, like *The Wizard of Oz* and the McLean County Fair.

At the time, this surprised me because Clara herself was an indifferent student, with grades hovering in the high C to low B neighborhood. Not that she wasn't smart — *she was!* But Clara always had so many other projects she was working on: building a diorama of our street; making a Halloween costume out of papier-mâché; trying to re-create the fabled Peanut Buster Parfait we once got by mistake when the counter girl at Dairy Queen misheard my order for a vanilla custard split two ways.

So it surprised me even more when, moments later, Clara announced her plan to run for class president.

"Wouldn't that be *so* cool?" Clara said, holding her fork loosely like an elongated index finger. "To run for president of my class?"

"I think that's a lot of work," I said, knowing nothing of student government except that my sister's plan to run for seventh-grade class president could complicate *my* plan to begin sixth grade in the same school as quietly as possible.

"I mean," I continued lamely, "I think you have to go to meetings after school and collect canned goods and —"

"Well, I think it's a *wonderful* idea!" Mom said. "Of course Clara should run for class president."

"You'll need a campaign slogan," Dad said, clearing the dishes from the table before some of us were even finished eating.

I listened from my bedroom upstairs as Mom, Dad, and Clara worked together at the dining room table, trying out various campaign themes.

Vote Clara Harrisong for 7th-Grade President! To the point, but a little dull.

Clara for President! Simple and friendly.

"I've got it!" Dad said. "I'll make some yard signs. I've got a bunch of scrap plywood in the shop. On one side of the signs we'll paint 'Clara's the Answer!' in big letters. On the other side we'll write 'What was the question?'"

"Funny, but a little flip," Mom said. "Clara doesn't want people to think she's not taking the election seriously. How about 'Pick Clara for President!' We'll cut flowers out of construction paper and make buttons. Get it? *Pick* Clara. Like you pick a flower?"

"Yeah," agreed Dad. "That's good. I could cut the yard signs with a jigsaw."

"Make them flowers!" said Mom. "Cut the signs in the shape of flowers, like daisies. Or tulips!"

"I could do a whole bunch of different flowers," Dad said. "Like one of those Pick-Me-Up bouquets."

I could hear the hesitation in Clara's response. Already she was somewhere else.

"I like those slogans," she said. "I mean, they're really good. But I want to think of something *great*. I've got plenty of time."

Later that night, I heard Mom talking to Clara in her room. Clara shared a bedroom with Laura down a short hall from mine and Ben's. Sally slept in a tiny dressing room off my parents' bedroom.

"You need to think about what you're offering your classmates," Mom was saying solemnly. "Think what sets you apart from the other kids who'll be running."

*   *   *

When I came down to breakfast the next morning, Clara was back at the dining room table, sketching block letters on a piece of yellow construction paper.

VOTE CLARA HARRISONG
7th-Grade President
for a
POSITIVE WAY of THINKING!

The last line was written in fat, hippie letters filled with smiley faces. Each face was topped with a jumble of dark curls, Clara's trademark.

"Hey, that looks like you!" said Ben, standing at the side of her chair. He was wearing his beloved Spider-Man pajamas and eating a banana.

"Does it?" asked Clara. "Okay, here's you."

On a piece of red construction paper, Clara drew a hilariously accurate picture of Ben in the mad scientist getup he'd worn last Halloween.

"Hey!" Ben marveled, his head cocked to one side, "Can I *have* that?"

"Sure," Clara said, handing the illustration to Ben, who took off in a blur.

"Maaa-ooom!" Ben yelled up the backstairs. "Look at this picture Clara drawed of me! Will you pin it on me so I can wear it?"

He did wear it on a T-shirt — well, for an hour or so — until it blew out the car window on their way to Bargain Bonanza to buy poster board for Clara's campaign.

I stayed home to look at my new notebooks.

*   *   *

Like Clara, I was an indifferent student. But unlike hers, my grades were embarrassingly good. Yes, a straight-A report card could make *The Most Embarrassing Things in My Life* list when the teacher's comments included things like: *"Sometimes I just want to tickle Charles to make him laugh!"*

Now *there* was an image that could keep a person awake all night. *Being tickled by a teacher?* Surely she didn't really mean that. So what was there to laugh about? Besides my family.

I never asked, but I'm guessing it was that cursed *tickle* note that prompted my mom to sign me up for Boy Scout camp in July.

"Honey, look," Mom said, showing me the sepia-tinted Summer Means Scouting! brochure with all those laughing Scouts on the front. "Hiking, canoeing, swimming, camping, archery, crafts, sing-alongs. It looks like so much *fun,* doesn't it? And I bet there'll be boys there from other elementary schools who'll be starting junior high with you."

I attended that hellish Boy Scout camp courtesy of a scholarship established by some rich guy in Chicago who had made millions off a chain of discount pharmacies. He believed Scouting, not the millions, made him "the man I am today!"

I'm sure he would've been thrilled to learn his "scholar" almost failed the only test they gave at camp. (And it was a *written* swimming test.)

Anything was better than Boy Scout camp, even school.

Truth is, I almost enjoyed the annual back-to-school ritual of piling all those new, plain-colored (*always* plain solid colors) Mead notebooks on my bed and deciding which color notebook to use for which subject.

I then returned to the age-old question of whether to write *Charles* (the name my parents called me) or *Charlie* (my nickname at school) on the cover of each notebook. Of course my handwriting — tiny, unreadable lines scratched hard on the paper until it sometimes tore through — couldn't be trusted with such tasks. I decided to ask Clara to write my name for me. She had this jangly way of printing letters that could make any name, even *Charles,* look cool.

I knew Charlie was a lighter, breezier, happier name. But it wasn't me. Like it or not, I was Charles Harrisong.

5.

The poster board mission took longer than expected. Bargain Bonanza was out of the white 22″ × 28″ sign boards. But Clara remembered having seen poster board at Miller Pharmacy, so the search party pressed onward: Mom, Clara, Ben, Laura, and Sally. Dad had the very convenient excuse of building a garage for someone across town.

When the others had been gone for more than an hour and the *Saturday Movie Matinee* on Channel 31 (*Lost Horizon*) failed to interest me, I decided to make popcorn and luxuriate in the rare delight of having the house to myself.

The afternoon sky was a greenish black. A violent storm was rolling through Normal, bringing terrific crashes of thunder and adding the drama I longed for on those late summer afternoons. I was always waiting for something — an adventure, an encounter, an authentic little miracle — to transform my ordinary life into something extraordinary.

It was pouring rain when the station wagon pulled into the driveway. Ben, Laura, and Sally squealed with delight as they ran through the puddles to the back door. With a stack of poster board on top of her head, like an oversized graduation mortarboard, Clara sprinted in the house and up to her room. I followed her there with my popcorn.

Though my older sister was a certified goof and an almost endless source of embarrassment to me (*"Hey Chums, look at this cool skirt I made out of Dad's old jeans!"*), our relationship had always been easy. Because we weren't interested in the same things — Clara liked art projects; I preferred watching TV and reading — we were spared the competition that many brothers and sisters face.

Plus, without ever talking about it, Clara and I both knew the financial situation at our house was dicey at best. Rather than compete for limited resources, Clara and I tried to present a unified front to our parents, asking for one thing to share — a rock tumbler, an ant farm, a VCR — instead of the things we really wanted: an artist's easel; my *own* room with a desk.

Poster board, of course, was another matter. It was inexpensive. And it was for the greater good of Clara's plan To Run For President of Her Class! I saw my mother write those very words in a note to my grandmother in Springfield earlier that morning. *Clara Is Going To Run For President of Her Class!*

Clara's bed and floor were covered with the drying poster boards. I cleared a place on the floor to sit, and set the bowl of popcorn next to an open sketch pad where *Positive Way of Thinking* was written in various lettering styles: block, script, thin line, and the jangly style I liked.

Of course her campaign platform would be positive thinking. Over the summer, Clara had been on a spiritual quest. First she became an atheist. Then an agnostic. Then a secular humanist. Then an Emersonian transcendentalist. I lost track after that. I think Clara did, too. She finally ended up believing in, as she put it, "the *awesome* power of positive thinking."

"Hey, Clara," I said. "When you have a second, can you write my name on my notebooks for me?"

She was returning from the bathroom and had a faded orange towel wrapped around her wet hair. She carried a Miracle Whip jar filled with water and paintbrushes.

"Yeah, no prob," she said, grabbing a handful of popcorn before climbing a stepladder at the end of Laura's bed.

Clara had spent much of July and August stenciling an intricate border of pastel rabbits just under the ceiling. It was her birthday present to Laura. Clara always gave great gifts. She had this knack for knowing just what people really wanted. I, on the other hand, had given Laura five yardsticks of gum (two grape, two bubble, one banana), all of which were leaning — still in their wrappers — in the corner against the radiator.

The upstairs windows were open, letting in a warm, earthy breeze that smelled like wet summer dirt before it becomes mud. It wasn't even four o'clock in the afternoon, but the storm had turned the sky dark.

Clara was working by the light of her mushroom-shaped candles from Wicks'n'Sticks. Her jasmine incense was burning in a cracked coffee cup, sending up a ribbon of white smoke.

"Feels like church in here," I said.

"*Better* than church," Clara said, facing the wall and fixing a smudged bunny ear with her thumb. "A million times better than church."

She jumped off the stepladder and grabbed another handful of popcorn.

"So, Clara," I said, watching her tilt her head to study the bunny border. "Tell me the truth. You really don't believe in God?"

"Mmmmmiyunno," she said, her mouth half-filled with popcorn. She swallowed before elaborating. "Do I *really* believe in God, or don't I? I mean, I do and I don't. And sometimes — don't get mad — but sometimes I say things just to give us something new to talk about at dinner. And to freak Mom and Dad out a little."

We both laughed. The thing was, Mom and Dad had been surprisingly okay with all of Clara's conversions and blasphemies, including the previous Sunday's, when she said after Mass that she thought the Dalai Lama was "ten times holier" than the Pope.

"The Dalai Lama's whole thing is just being *kind*," Clara had explained at dinner that night. "He said that his true religion is *kindness*. Isn't that *great?*"

"I like that," Dad said. He had made his famous pizza (*"It's da Papa-pizza!"*), a messy marriage of flattened refrigerator rolls topped with spaghetti sauce and cheese and baked on a cookie sheet.

"You just have to try to be kind and that's enough," said Clara, watching Dad remove the molten mass from the oven.

"I don't know if that's enough," said Mom. She was centering the pizza bread on the cutting board for Dad to slice. "I think God expects more of us than just being nice."

"Like what?" Clara asked.

"Well," Mom said, "for one thing, I think you should be grateful for all you've been given."

"I *am* grateful," said Clara. "But I don't have to go to church to be grateful. I can be grateful right here at home while I'm listening to music or painting."

"I think you have to find a place to be quiet," Dad said, distributing the gloppy masses of pizza onto our plates. "To think about things. That's why I like church. But if church doesn't do that for you —"

"We don't have to go to church anymore!" Ben proclaimed, standing on his chair, holding his milk glass over his head in victory.

I watched Mom clench her teeth and shoot daggers with her eyes at Dad. I remember thinking: *She's mad at him. I can tell just by her jaw that she's mad.* I used my secret gift to hear the unspoken between my parents. It chilled me to discover this underworld that lurked below the surface; the dark adult world of accusation and guilt that dwelt in tight jaws and cold, hardened glares and unfinished conversations. (*"Sure, it'll work! You just gotta give it time and believe in —"* *"Drive, Frank. Can you please just drive?"*)

*   *   *

The bunny smudge was fixed. Clara filled her cupped hands with popcorn and flopped cross-legged on Laura's bed.

"I guess I just don't believe in the same God that Mom and Dad do," Clara said. "An old white guy with a beard? I just don't buy that. I don't need it. I see God in so many other places."

She paused to remove from her mouth an unpopped

kernel. She looked at it and then tossed it across the room toward her closet.

"I mean, I s'pose I do feel Him — or Her — or Something inside me," she continued, crawling off the bed and onto the floor. She scooped up another fistful of popcorn from the bowl.

"And whatever it is," she said, between bites, "that's what I try to see in other people. Because I know when I think the best of people, they think the best of me back. And when I try not to judge people, I don't feel like people are judging me."

She looked quizzically at the popcorn in her right hand. "Chumsley, did you put something weird on this?"

Shoot. I knew I'd put on too much.

"I sprinkled some of that Lawry's Seasoned Salt stuff on it. Sorry."

"No, I like it." She stuffed a handful in her mouth and crunched loudly. "I meant weird *good.* Not weird bad."

She grabbed more.

"So," Clara said, returning by stepladder to the plucky rabbits marching across the ceiling, "I guess I just believe in kindness more than in God. Or I believe kindness *is* God. Oh, Chums, I don't know what I believe. But I definitely believe in thinking the *best* about everyone. Because when you look for the best in people, that's what you see."

On *see,* a thunderbolt *BASHED* somewhere across town. The sound made me jump.

Not Clara. She threw her head back, tossed a piece of popcorn in the air and caught it in her mouth, like a happy seal, and continued painting bunnies.

6.

Ben was almost right: We didn't have to go to church anymore. At Clara's urging, my parents agreed to develop a new commandment regarding the worship of higher deities.

The new rule at our house was thus: Thou shalt attend a weekly religious service until the age of eighteen. It didn't have to be at St. Jude's. It didn't even have to be at a Catholic church. But if you went somewhere other than St. Jude's, you had to give a report about it at dinner. (My mother was no fool.)

On Sunday, Clara rode her purple Stingray to a spirituality service ("They don't call it *Mass*") held in Normal's shabbiest strip mall, where the congregants sat on metal folding chairs, and Lark, the Vision Leader, conducted guided imagery sessions.

I didn't go with Clara, even though part of me agreed with her about church. Some of those Bible stories just didn't add up, I thought, as I sat daydreaming through the 10:45 guitar Mass at St. Jude's with the rest of my family. People living to be seven hundred years old? God asking that poor father with two sons to kill one of them? And then telling him, just in the nick of time, that He was *kidding?* (That God! What a sense of humor!)

And the bit about Noah. He *really* found exactly two — one male, one female — of every animal? Two wildebeests? Two ring-necked pheasants? Two giant papillon rabbits? And nothing extra, not even a little baby gerbil, snuck on at the last minute? Come on.

I knew parts of the Bible, like the parables, were stories Jesus told to teach a lesson. My problem was, I couldn't tell which were the real parts of the Bible and which were the made-up stories. Adam and Eve? Salome dancing around with John the Baptist's head on a plate?

Who wrote this stuff? And whoever it was, why didn't they put the made-up stuff in a different-colored ink? Or, if that was too expensive, just print it in *italics.*

Lot's wife looked back from behind him, *and she became a pillar of salt.*

On the other hand, I wasn't nearly as brave as Clara. Because maybe it *was* all true. And if it was, why mess around with it? Plagues? Leprosy? And, of course, the biggie: *getting nailed to a cross.* While your Father stands by and does nothing? (That God. What a pal!)

And he that curseth his father, or his mother, shall surely be put to death.

So my point was simply this: Why not try to believe a little? Just in case. Just enough to pass the final exam. Besides, I didn't think going to church was all that terrible. Give me St. Jude's any day over Bargain Bonanza.

The funny thing was, when I pictured God, I often thought of Bargain Bonanza. To me, God was like the real founder of Bargain Bonanza. He created it, but He didn't shop there. He didn't need any of the stuff down here. But He knew there were people like my family who needed Bargain Bonanza.

He knew there would always be people who lived far from big cities and fancy shopping malls made of mirrored glass; people who would never buy a suit in London or shoes in Italy. Some of us needed Wranglers, by God. He knew this. And we were the people He *really* loved.

(Okay, He was God. So He loved everyone.)

But surely He had a special place in His heart for people like us who wandered for years, lost in the middle of nowhere. He understood what it was like down here. It was like Lent *all the time.*

That was a Ben-ism, coined while cleaning closets when he was six.

"Is it Lent?" my brother had asked Mom. "Because this sure feels like Lent."

Clara and I used the expression a lot. While scrubbing a crusty casserole dish, or trying to tame the angry bushes in front of our house on one of those godforsakenly hot August days, one of us would turn off the water tap or drop the hedge clippers in exhaustion and ask: "Hey, is this Lent? 'Cause this sure feels like Lent."

But surely God knew what we were going through. If anyone knew what summers in central Illinois were like, God did. And He was going to make it worth our while in the long run.

It was the short run that was tough. And in Normal, Illinois, even the short run seemed long. Because these were the dog days of summer, when God was in semiretirement. And somehow, those smirky guys in middle management at Bargain Bonanza had taken over the day-to-day operations. The same guys who came up with the idea of decorating discount stores with hay bales.

These were the men responsible for renovating our church. The ones who made the decision to cover the marble floors with orange carpeting; replace the wooden pews with fake wood "family prayer benches"; and hang a huge *Star Trek*-y light fixture over the altar, where Bible verses (IN THE BEGINNING WAS THE WORD, AND THE WORD WAS WITH GOD, AND THE WORD WAS GOD) and friendly reminders

(HAS YOUR FAMILY RESERVED A TABLE FOR MONTE CARLO NIGHT?) scrolled during Mass.

The first time we went back to St. Jude's after the Grand Renovation (capital expense fund-raising theme: *Redecorating Our Church Home in the Image of God's House*), my sister Laura said, "Oh, my gosh! It looks like Pizza Hut in here!"

It was the perfect description of the renovated church, now completely lacking in the gloomy dignity I happened to like.

Somehow I knew God wasn't much for pricey liturgical light fixtures. That's why He'd decided not to work out of the Bargain Bonanza company headquarters in Dallas. Truth of the matter was, He found the corporate offices flashy and offensive.

"And those conference rooms!" He'd say to Himself on the flight home. *"In my day, we didn't need conference rooms that size!"*

God much preferred the office He'd built on a secret floor hidden above Bargain Bonanza. From there, He could look down and watch for shoplifters. Sometimes He'd make a note of it in one of the Big Chief notebooks on his desk. But most times, He'd just yawn and say to Himself: *Kid stealing black licorice in aisle 4. No harm, no foul.* (Like me, God refused to use those cheeseball aisle names — in this case, the Good Grub & Sweet Snax aisle.)

Of course God could see the violators. He was God! He saw everything. But what did He care?

"Kid, if you're hungry, go get some of those fresh dough-nut holes in the bakery department," He'd whisper to a young shoplifter. "Now *those* are good. And grab some cheese and yogurt, too. Something with a little protein in it."

Then He might doodle for a while. And then He'd close his eyes and take a long nap.

That's what I believed about God. As much as I believed anything.

7.

School started on the last Monday in August. Four Normal elementary schools (K–5) fed into Normal Junior High (6–8), home of the Fighting Panthers! Much of the first week of sixth grade was spent on something called *icebreakers*, painfully laborious games designed by school administrators to introduce students from the various schools to one another.

Far more impressive — from a management perspective, anyway — was the student-organized Pick Your Clique program. Of course it was a misnomer. One didn't *pick* his or her clique. One was *picked* by the universally acknowledged clique leaders whose reputations were established and unchallenged by the third day of school.

The air-conditioning at Normal Junior High was on the blink the entire first week. The classrooms were so hot, students were allowed to wear shorts to school.

I passed on the shorts option (my skinny white legs having recently been added to my *Ways My Body Is Weird* list) and alternated between jeans and khakis. Most days I was the only one in Mrs. Johnson's sixth-grade class wearing long pants.

"Charlie, how in the *world* can you wear jeans?" my new classmates asked approximately seven hundred times a day that first week. "Aren't you *melting?*"

No, no, I assured them. I was fine. And I was. The eighty-degree indoor temperatures at school weren't a shock to my system since we didn't have air-conditioning at home — just fans. I made the mistake of telling my classmates this on Friday after lunch.

"What?!" demanded Victor Wolfe, a swaggering clique leader from Carl Sandburg Elementary whose claim to fame was that he had been picked up by the Normal cops over the summer for setting kittens on fire with gasoline.

"How can you not have *air-conditioning?*" Victor snarled. "Don't you know your brain can actually *boil* if it gets too hot? Why don't you have air-conditioning at your house?"

I started to explain that it wasn't exactly *our* house.

"They just *rent* it," offered Brenda Harris in an annoyingly buoyant tone. Brenda's locker had been next to mine at Normal Elementary.

"What?!" Victor asked with a wide-open laugh. "Why don't your parents just *buy* a house and put in air-conditioning? We rent *cars* when we go on vacation. But nobody rents a *house!* Why do you *rent* your house?"

Brenda helpfully explained it was because we had such a big family. Five kids and all.

"*What?!*" Victor snorted at me. (*Oh, he was on a roll now!*) "Why do you have so many kids in your family? Why didn't your parents have just one or two kids? Or at most, *three*. That way, they could've *bought* a house *with air-conditioning* and —"

My boiling brain could absorb no more. Besides, I thought: *Where is Mrs. Johnson?* And why must there always be so much free time for this idle chitchat? Wasn't there a U.S. Constitution we should be memorizing? Or some long, boring poems we could read together as a class?

But on a deeper level I thought: *He's right. Why don't we have air-conditioning? Why don't we own our house? Why don't we have a normal-sized family? What were my parents thinking? Was anyone paying attention?*

And where the heck *was* Mrs. Johnson? Our teacher had mysteriously disappeared from the classroom. I could hear her talking — now giggling — in the hallway.

Then I saw them: mothers. A whole flock of them, standing out in the hallway, whispering. My mom was there, too. (And what was she wearing? A patchwork dress made from my discarded Bargain Bonanza neckerchiefs? With one of Dad's belts around it? Oh, God.)

The mothers held Tupperware containers and Dixie cups and jumbo cans of Hi-C punch. They counted among themselves ("One, two, three . . .") and then stormed into the classroom.

Mrs. Johnson, who raced in front of them, now stood in front of the blackboard with her hands on her hips, pretending to be surprised. "Well, hello, ladies," she said primly. "What's going on here?"

"You've heard of pop quizzes?" said the mother-in-charge, as if reading from a script. (*Had they rehearsed this little stunt?*) "Well, this is a pop *party!*"

I immediately thought of Ben and how much he would've loved this. My mom smiled at me, subtly, which I appreciated.

But still, there it was. And there we were. Mom in one of her homemade outfits (*Please don't let her have a matching scarf that goes with this getup*), holding a bag of Cowboy Cal's Cow Patty Melt Cookies.

Mrs. Johnson was saying something about a new program in the Normal Public School System designed to make the classroom an environment for "self-discovery in a context of joyful play because learning is, at its core, an exploration and a celebration of the light within us, shining brightly in the fog of —"

I stopped listening when I saw the mothers piling brightly wrapped gifts on Mrs. Johnson's desk. She saw them, too.

"Ladies," Mrs. Johnson said, her head cocked at an almost right angle to her body, "I hope those are for the entire class."

The mothers giggled.

"No," the mother-in-charge sang. "They're for *you!* Just some little back-to-school goodies."

"Don't worry," a frumpy mother added. "We had a five-dollar limit."

The mother-in-charge smiled icily at the frumpy mother.

"Really, they're not from us at all," the mother-in-charge explained. "They're from your students, who are *SO* lucky to have *SUCH* a wonderful teacher like you this year. *RIGHT,* children?"

My class responded with a robotic, "Uh-huh."

And then the mothers scampered away. My mom looked at me and did something with her eyes that was a cross between a wink and a wince. I watched her in the hallway tie a neckerchief around her head as a scarf.

Mrs. Johnson began opening her gifts in front of the class. A coffee mug. A magnetic memo pad. Another coffee mug. A fountain pen. (Now *that* was the perfect gift for a teacher.) A bookmark. A tin of oatmeal cookies.

"This looks interesting, Charles," she said, when she came to my gift. She carefully tore the canary yellow wrapping paper covered with the (*Oh, for God's sake*) pink dancing pigs. "What could it be?"

I felt the muscles in my neck tighten. What *could* it be? I had no earthly idea. And why hadn't Mom *asked* me what I wanted to get my teacher? We definitely should have discussed this.

The obvious choice would have been a book. Or better yet, a gift certificate to a bookstore. Or a gift certificate to the mall. Something generic that wouldn't call attention to itself or the alleged giver.

Or no gift at all! Hey, *that* would've been okay. Were the other boys in my class giving Mrs. Johnson a gift? No. None of their mothers had taken part in this madcap prank. None of them had gifts for Mrs. Johnson. Just Jason Underwood. (And of course *he* would. He wet his *pants* in third grade!) And me.

I was in the red zone on the embarrassment scale, and Mrs. Johnson hadn't even opened the gift.

Why hadn't I been clearer with Mom when she'd asked if I wanted her to be a sixth-grade room mother? *Not only do I not want you to be a room mother, I don't want you to step foot inside my school! Ever. This is junior high! And I'm trying to start over. I'm trying to BE Normal.* That's what I should've said. Instead of: "No thanks, Mom."

Mrs. Johnson was now folding the dancing pig wrapping paper. (*"This will be adorable on my decoupage trunk."*) That's when I saw the purple plastic bottle. The label on the front pictured a cheesy knight — in armor! — with his long-lashed eyes closed. He was bowing his head and kneeling in front of a beautiful maiden with cascading tendrils that reached the floor. The knight was presenting her with — *what?!* — *a bottle of foaming bath oil?* Did they even *have* foaming bath oil back then?

"Oh, Charles!" Mrs. Johnson said, cradling the plastic bottle with both hands and showing it to the class. "I love Night to Remember bath oil! How in the world did you know?"

My face burned. I could hear the first lone giggle behind me. (*Victor Wolfe?*) I felt it as it swelled like a tidal wave into an enormous undulating all-class laugh-fest.

This is not happening, I said to myself. *This Is Not Happening.*

But of course it was. And of course an hour later during Language Arts, we started a unit on King Arthur and the Knights of the Round Table. Mrs. Johnson asked me to pass out the workbooks.

"Because you're my knight in shining armor, Charles," she said. "I just love Night to Remember!"

Once again I heard a snickering across the room. I felt it build into a rollicking wave of laughter. Then the dam burst; the levee failed.

"What?" asked Mrs. Johnson, watching the entire class (minus one) roar with delight. "Just what is so darn funny?"

Which of course only made it funnier to my classmates. I walked unsteadily across the front of the room, first counting and then distributing the correct number of workbooks for each row. I felt like I was surfing through a monsoon of laughter. Even Jason Underwood was laughing, *the traitor.*

I could taste the bitter embarrassment in my mouth. I could feel myself drowning in the air-less air.

I hadn't thought of that feeling — drowning on dry land, waves crashing in your head and your chest — since that stupid Boy Scout camp. It was hard to breathe, not just in the lake, but everywhere.

Before a Scout could go swimming, he had to pass a class called Don't Drown! The Importance of Water Safety. Mr. Breedlove, the district scoutmaster, taught the class, which he renamed Only Dummies Drown. According to Mr. Breedlove, all you had to do to avoid drowning was remember a few simple things, which he conveniently arranged to form the word *DUMMY*: **D**on't *swim alone; always swim with a fellow Scout.* **U**nderstand *your swimming limitations and stay within them.* **M**ake *sure you swim in supervised areas only and obey all "No Diving" signs.* And so forth.

"Kid stuff," Mr. Breedlove said. "Only a dummy could flunk this."

But when he passed out the tests, a wave of panic crashed over me. I couldn't breathe. I couldn't think right. I overcompensated by offering up a litany of possibilities for every letter in DUMMY: *Do wear a life jacket! Don't panic! Decide in advance if going swimming is really necessary. Don't stay with a sinking boat! (Unless an adult tells you to.)*

In the space reserved for five answers (one D, one U, two M's and a Y), I crammed in close to thirty, with sentences snaking around the page in my crazy old-man handwriting: *Don't try to help a drowning person (Unless you know what you're doing); 'Member you can drown in just one inch of water; Y risk death? Wait one hour after meals before swimming.*

I passed the test only because it was pass/fail. When Mr. Breedlove handed back the papers, he looked at me (the scholarship kid!), threw my test at me like a Frisbee, and said under his breath, *"Jeeeeezus."*

I got in the water exactly once that week when we had our official troop photo taken on the diving platform, out in the middle of the murky lake. We had to swim to get there.

We got the pictures back on the last day of camp. I was surprised to see that all the other boys were smiling with their mouths hanging open like happy dogs, as if someone had just uncorked the funniest joke of the year. It was clear from my face — serious as a pilgrim — that I had either not heard or not understood the punch line.

This was the flip side to my secret power of being able to see and hear things that other people couldn't. Often I missed things — embarrassingly simple stuff like knock-knock jokes and true/false questions (*"All drowning deaths are preventable. T or F"*) — that other people got easily.

But Night to Remember I understood. I got the joke. It was on me. Or, more to the point, it *was* me. Me and my family. *Pick Your Clique!* I had picked mine, all right. No, I had been picked by the Harrisong clique, whose members wore clown clothes and lived in the creepy cartoon house behind the Tasmanian devil-y bushes that bore a striking re- semblance to our possessed hair.

As for my secret power, I never added it to *The Most Em- barrassing Things in My Life* list because I didn't know what to call it. Besides, it wasn't a thing. It was who I was. I hid it from my family, like I hid that stupid camp photo, which I buried in the bottom of my suitcase. I didn't think about it again until the night we left.

8.

Like a baseball manager readjusting his starting lineup, I constantly revised *The Most Embarrassing Things in My Life* list, giving up sentimental all-stars (That Time in Third Grade When I Pronounced the "C" in Tucson During the Geography Bee) to make room for ambitious rookies like Night to Remember bath oil.

After that first long week of school, it seemed appropriate to compile a *Most Embarrassing Things in My Life* list: *The Back-to-School Edition.* Inspired by Scoutmaster Breedlove, I confined my list to words that began with M, E, T, I, M, L, L, T, B, T, S, and E. This worked nicely because the perennial list-topper was always **M**y Family.

Which is not to say I didn't love my family. Of course I did. But **L**ove was number six on the list. **E**mbarrassing Things My Family Did was number two.

I made a sub-list of *Embarrassing Things My Family Did.* The fact that we Always Did Everything Together was number one on that list. So then I made a sub-sub-list of *Things We Always Did Together:* going to Pizza Hut for dinner; bike riding; playing board games; trick or treating; cleaning out the garage; shopping for underwear. Each of which begat their own sub-sub-lists and sub-sub-sub-lists.

At least making lists was something I could do alone.

Even Clara's election was becoming Something We Did Together. We talked about the campaign endlessly at dinner. How do you file with the election officials? (Clara: "I think I just tell the school secretary, Miss Phillips, and she puts my name on a list.") When's election day? (Clara: "Friday, September 14.") How many other kids are running? (Clara: "So far, five. But more kids will probably sign up next week.")

My dad was now wearing a POSITIVE WAY OF THINKING construction paper button on his work shirts. Ben had CLARA FOR PREZ!!! scratched all over his notebooks.

Of course I wanted Clara to win the election. But I couldn't wear those dopey buttons she made. I was a sixth grader! And besides, all that togetherness was choking me. I needed to do something alone.

On Saturday morning of Labor Day weekend, I devised a modest plan.

"Mom, okay if I go see a movie?" I asked, real casual like, in the voice I used when asking if I could have some crackers before dinner. "I can just ride my bike over to the movie theater. Just me."

"What movie would you like to see, honeybunch?" Mom

said. She was pulling wet laundry out of the washing machine and dumping it in the dryer.

I told her the name of a movie I'd heard kids talking about at school.

"What's it about?" she asked.

"A spacecraft from another planet filled with extraterrestrial dogs that lands on Earth and how these dogs take over the government in Washington, D.C."

"Hmmmmm," Mom said, turning the dryer on. I could hear the rivets in somebody's jeans hitting the sides of the dryer: *clack clack clack clack clack clack.*

"Extraterrestrial dogs," she repeated, louder, to compensate for the noise. "Does that sound good?"

Oh yeah! I assured her. It was really good!

"I wonder if Ben would like it," she continued.

I assured her that he wouldn't. No. Definitely not.

Clara and Laura, taking a break from roller skating up and down the driveway, walked by the laundry room.

"Hey, are you guys talking about that dogs-from-outer-space movie?" Clara asked.

"Yes," Mom said. "Does it hold any interest for you two?"

"Of course!" said Laura. "It's *supposubly* hilarious! Can we see it? Pleeeeeeeeeeease?"

"We'll talk about it," Mom said in her *nobody-get-your-hopes-up* voice.

At lunch, while dropping a handful of Corny Cal corn chips next to my egg salad sandwich, Mom said, "Charles, tell Dad about the movie we were talking about."

I did.

Dad said, between bites, "Extraterrestrial dogs in the White House? That *does* sound good. What do you say we treat ourselves to a night out? One last hurrah before summer ends."

He clapped his hands together once, loudly, like an exclamation point, before asking, "How's tonight look for everybody?"

And so we went to dinner at Pizza Hut and then to the movie. All seven of us.

The last movie we had seen (together, of course!) was in July, right before I left for camp. It was *Cinderella*. During the scene where the birds carry the ribbons in their little beaks and create a ball gown for the heroine, Laura said — and not in a whisper — "Look at *that!* I want a bird that'll make a dress for *me!*"

The people behind us burst into laughter, prompting Laura to burst into tears ("They're *laughing* at me. Why does everybody always have to *laugh* at me?"), prompting Mom to take Laura into the lobby to explain a) that the people behind us weren't laughing at her, and b) the magic of animation.

On the drive home, Mom posed her favorite question: "Why don't we all go around and say one thing we learned from that movie?"

When it was Laura's turn, she grumbled between sniffles, "I hated those stupid *fake* birds."

But that was over a month ago. Laura was six now, as she liked to tell people — the mailman, gas station attendants, her dolls — and, as far as I knew, there were no birds in this movie. Maybe we were in luck.

Mom packed Bargain Bonanza–brand sandwich cookies (Cowboy Cal's Favorites!) in plastic bags secured with green twist ties. Four vanilla sandwich cookies per bag per child. We drove to the theater in our powder blue station wagon. We sat together in the center section of the theater, halfway back from the screen. Every time a dog appeared in the movie, Sally looked, pointed, and yelled, "Big Dog! Look at the Big Funny Dog!"

A group of boys from my class were at the same movie (of course they were!), sitting in the last row of the theater, eating from huge barrels of popcorn and oversized boxes of chocolate-covered raisins. And laughing! Laughing!

I sat, eating my four cookies and watching stone-faced as the extraterrestrial dogs dressed in three-piece blue-striped suits took over Washington, D.C. Once in office, the dogs threw all the cats in jail and passed inane laws, mandating "people pooper-scoopers." Every time a dog said this — *people pooper-scooper* — my classmates howled with laughter.

I hated that my mom and sisters were hearing this phrase. (*Poop, butt,* and *shut up* were considered bad words at our house.) I also hated that my dad was sitting at the end of our row, snoring. I couldn't blame him. The movie wasn't the least bit funny. It didn't even make sense. When the dog president ate the poisoned dog biscuit, the dog *vice* president should've become president — not the *cat* who lost the election and was sulking in prison on *feline*-y charges.

Why did everything have to be so stupid?

And why had I wanted to see this cheesy Bargain Bonanza–grade movie? My dad must've thought I was an idiot. But that was my point! They didn't have to come with me. Why did we have to do everything *together?* And why did my classmates have to be at the same movie? At least Victor Wolfe wasn't there.

I tried to slip out of the theater unnoticed, but the boys from my class were in the lobby (*Oh, of course! There's Victor Wolfe! With a girl?!*), horsing around in their cooler-than-thou way. They noticed me with the same enthusiasm I'd notice a dirty penny on the sidewalk.

"Oh, hey, it's Charlie Harrisong."

"Hi, Charlie."

"Hey, Harrisong, you big *people pooper-scooper!*"

They collapsed as one in a spastic fit of uncontrollable laughter. I smiled — mouth closed — and lifted my hand in a casual wave.

I was careful not to look too interested or eager. Or even troubled by the fact that six — no wait, not six, eight (EIGHT!) — boys in my class had gotten together to see this movie. These things didn't just organize themselves. Oh, no. Someone called someone. And then someone called someone else. And then someone's parents had to drive them all here and then pick them up. No, they'd probably just ridden their bikes. Just another little adventure! No big deal. And all of this had transpired without anyone ever thinking to ask me to join them.

Me. Mister Irrelevant. Clique-free Charlie!

Oh, who cared? My mom probably wouldn't have let me go with them, anyway. Not without a parental chaperone. We didn't *do* that kind of thing in *our* clique. Still, this was not a disaster. At least I was wearing long pants. (And to think how close I'd come to wearing those comfortable cut-offs!) Not even close to the red zone. Just get out of the theater before —

Dad was walking into the lobby, hand in hand with Sally. They were passing right in front of my classmates.

Please, God. Let them keep walking. Just keep walking. Don't say anything. Keep walking. Don't —

"Well," Dad said in a voice like a Roman orator. "This has certainly been a night to remember!"

I gave up on God. Or at least on the idea of God as an aggressive manager with a passion for details (*"Get me that Harrisong file. NOW!"*).

Apparently God had grown tired of the whole thing. Well? Think how old He was. I was only eleven and already I knew how He felt.

*   *   *

"What's wrong, Chumsley?" Clara asked on the drive home. We were in the backseat. Laura was between us, sleeping. Sally was in the front seat, between Mom and Dad. Ben was playing with his action figures in the tiny carpeted cargo area behind the backseat.

"Wrong?" I replied. "Everything. There wasn't one good thing in that whole movie."

"I didn't think it was that bad," Clara said, yawning, the shadows from the telephone poles rolling across her face every few seconds.

"Not that *bad?*"

I was incredulous. I was disgusted with myself and with the movie. And now this — from my older sister?

"It was awful," I said. *"People pooper-scoopers?* Was that supposed to be funny? It was one hundred percent stupid."

"Chums," she said, closing her eyes and resting her head against the armrest on her side of the car. "It was a movie about dogs from another planet taking over the White House. I mean, for what it was, it was okay."

"I *hated* it."

"You hate too much," she said. "Don't think so hard. Just relax."

Right. And just *BE NORMAL,* too, will you?

9.

The worst part about Labor Day was that it came after we'd already started school. When it arrived with that tease of a three-day weekend, it felt like summer was reasserting itself. If you weren't careful, you could almost believe that sweet summer had a fighting chance against the great and powerful fall.

On Sunday, after we got back from 10:45 Mass and Clara returned from her spirituality service (*"Lark gave me a dreamcatcher for good luck in the election!"*), she took Ben, Laura, and Sally to the Normal Community Center & Pool for one last swim of the season. Dad sent a five-dollar bill with Clara to buy ice cream for them all at the snack bar. I stayed home to read.

Like a cat, I'd always hated swimming, even before Boy Scout camp. "Except for whales, I don't think mammals are *supposed* to swim," I told my first swimming teacher when she told me I swam like a rock.

Plus, the pool was always so loud and crowded, with countless possible land mines. The locker room alone was a bottomless sea of potential catastrophes. Reading was much safer. It meant simply retreating to my bed, turning the box fan so it blew toward my face, and rereading one of the haunted house mysteries I'd loved since third grade.

They were the *Make Your Own Mystery* books with multiple story lines. On every page, the reader got to pick where to go next:

> **Care to peek behind the hidden wall in the library?**
>   **Proceed to page 47.**
> **Want to see what's up the back staircase?**
>   **Turn to page 52. (If you dare!)**
> **Crrrrreak!!! What's that under the loose floorboard?**
>   **Find out on page 53.**
> **Or, to follow the mysterious talking owl,**
>   **turn to page 54.**

God, I loved those books! No matter which page you turned to, there was a wonderful treasure waiting.

> **Look! There in the corner of the attic:**
>   **the missing trunk filled with gold coins!**
> **And in the top drawer lay the pale blue envelope**
>   **containing a crisp $1 million bill.**
> **Jewels, jewels, jewels! Everywhere she looked:**
>   **jewels!**

I kept those prized books on my bookshelf for Ben, though I don't think he ever read a single one of the garishly illustrated paperbacks with the mildly insulting POPULAR WITH EARLY AND RELUCTANT READERS! stickers on the back covers.

But I read them eagerly, passionately, over and over again. Sometimes I'd read the same book repeatedly until I'd explored every possible route. Other times I'd read my whole collection (there were only seven) and take all right turns. Or all left turns. Or the middle choice, from beginning to end, just to see if I could crack the code. I never did.

How did people write those books? The plots were so intricately woven; so complicated and yet seamless. I could never think of all those secret rooms filled with undeserved treasures. But maybe I could do a cheap knockoff version. Not the kind of books you buy in bookstores, but the Bargain Bonanza–brand books sold in bins. *The Abracadabra U-Decide Mystery Series, by Charles Harrisong. Three books for $5!*

My series would be a publishing phenomenon. Like the discount pharmacy baron in Chicago who sent me to Boy Scout camp, I'd use my book royalties to establish a scholarship program for kids. Only, my endowment would be for kids who didn't want to go to camp. I'd pay them to stay home all summer and read haunted house mysteries. I'd send them a box full of fresh new books every week. My parents would marvel at my quirky success.

"Have you seen Charles's new book?" they'd ask their friends at church. Maybe I'd even get some free publicity on the scrolling light fixture at St. Jude's. He gave them bread from heaven to eat. Book signing today at Bargain Bonanza! C. Harrison and the 37th Abracadabra U-Decide Mystery.

(Of course they'd still misspell our last name.)

My parents, by now old and wrinkled, would shuffle humbly along Dude Drive while I nervously scribbled lame inscriptions in the books for former teachers and neighbors.

> To Mrs. Johnson —
> Well, it's not King Arthur and the Round
> Table. But hope you enjoy it.
> With warm regards,
> Charles (Charlie) Harrisong
> P.S. Go Panthers!

My fantasy was interrupted when the swimmers returned home shortly after three o'clock.

"Danny Daltino threw a dirty diaper in the baby pool," Ben yelled from the kitchen.

Sure enough, and for all the wrong reasons, the pool

closed early for the year. Everyone was disappointed except Laura, who, during the evacuation, scored a sleepover invitation from a new school pal. From my bedroom I could hear her packing and discussing the logistics with Clara.

"And if I get scared in the middle of the night, I can just call — no matter what time — and Mom will come pick me up, right?"

"Right," Clara said. "You'll be okay."

Ben and a buddy were downstairs in the living room, practicing their sumo wrestling moves. Sally was playing dolls in the basement with Mom, who told everyone not to bother her because she had a summer's worth of ironing to do.

Clara was taking a break from making her Positive Thinking campaign propaganda. "I've already put up thirty posters," she'd told me that morning. "I don't want the other candidates to think I'm hogging all the bulletin boards."

So she was back to painting rabbits. The bunny border around the ceiling had been an enormous hit with Laura. She'd almost passed out with joy when Clara finished it.

"From now on I will *always* dream about rabbits because they'll be the last thing I see before I fall asleep!" Laura had said, holding both hands over her heart.

Now Clara was painting an entire rabbit mural on the wall next to Laura's bed. Ballerina rabbits. Princess rabbits. George and Martha Washington as rabbits. Our family as rabbits. The *Little House on the Prairie* family as rabbits. (Clara was reading these books to Laura.) A magician rabbit pulling a rabbit out of a hat.

While Clara painted, I grabbed my backpack and rode my bike over to Hollywood-At-Home Movies. The challenge in picking videos was to find movies that Mom would approve of, but not so much that she'd want to watch them *with* me. Hence, the Timeless Classics aisle, where ninety-nine cents rented five videos for three days. (I always liked the people at Hollywood-At-Home for tailoring their pricing plan to acknowledge that some of these classics were downright duds.)

I trawled the endlessly boring collection of black-and-white videos with their equally dull covers and chose my usual mix: A couple of Agatha Christie mysteries. A Hitchcock thriller. A silly Disney movie about a cat named Thomasina with a complicated inner life. Clara insisted it was her all-time favorite movie, though I don't think she ever actually watched the whole thing.

I was struggling to find a fifth movie worth lugging home when I picked up a video jacket that looked promising. At least it had a boy on the cover instead of one of those old-timey actresses who looked like the girls in my mom's high school yearbooks. I shuddered when I saw the title of the video in my hand: *The Yearling.*

As anyone in my fifth-grade class could've told you, I'd read *The Yearling*. (*"Did you hear what happened to Charlie Harrisong in Language Arts today? Did you HEAR? One minute he was just normal, reading his book, and then —"*)

I had no desire to see the movie version of *The Yearling*. None. I dropped the video like a snake back on its shelf and grabbed a boring-looking courtroom drama titled *To Kill a Mockingbird*.

When I got home, I carried the crummy kitchen television into the girls' bedroom. I lugged the VCR in there, too, and hooked it up.

Clara and I watched all five movies on Sunday and Monday. Rather, I watched them, lying on my stomach, eating mint chocolate chip ice cream. Clara listened while standing on Laura's bed and painting.

"Wait, I'm confused!" she said several times per movie.

I'd have to pause the tape and explain: "The lady thought she was in love with the handsome guy she met on the train, but now this mysterious stranger is making the moves on her and she's all confused."

"Okay," Clara said. "Got it. Keep going."

I'd hit the PLAY button, and Clara returned to her mural.

To Kill a Mockingbird was the only movie that Clara watched without painting. Now *there* was a movie! We watched it once on Sunday night and again on Labor Day

Monday. We loved everything about it. The opening credits (that gorgeous slow pan across the toys). The sad/happy music. Scout and Jem. Dill (those teeth!), who spent his summers next door to the Finches. The part where the rabid dog lumbers lopsidedly down the street and how Atticus nails him (One-shot Finch!). And, of course, Arthur Boo Radley, the spooky neighbor, who supposedly stabbed his father in the leg with a pair of scissors.

"Do you think people think of us as the Radleys?" I asked Clara during a snack break on Monday. I was refilling my ice-cream bowl. She was making a grilled peanut butter sandwich.

"Don't be crazy, Chums," Clara said, retying the red bandanna around her hair while a tiny button of peanut butter sizzled in the skillet. "Of course they don't."

"I don't know," I said. "Living in this old house. The weird yellow bricks. The creepy bushes. From the outside, it looks haunted."

"Haunted?" She laughed. "I never think of this house as scary."

Fearless Clara.

But I knew better. Before I fell asleep that night, I made a list of all the ways we were like the Radleys (*strange looking; live in a scary house; unintentionally entertaining to schoolchildren*), which begat a sub-list of all the ways I was like

Boo Radley (*shy; weird until you get to know him, then nice; gives gum as gifts to little kids*).

And then it was Tuesday morning and we had to go back to school. Summer was officially over; dismissed with a mean little shove by its replacement: fall.

10.

Third grade was turning out to be not as bad as Ben had predicted. He seemed to have an endless supply of friends who shared his interests (Japanese comics, anything Western, professional wrestling, plastic action figures) and sense of humor.

I learned that Ben was The Funny Kid in his class when I walked home from school behind him one day during the second week of school. He was shuffling along the sidewalk, telling his homemade jokes to a group of boys from his class.

"And then you won't believe what happened next," Ben said.

The group went silent. He had these kids in the palm of his hand. Then, with perfect comedic timing, Ben said, "They all *urinated* in their pants!"

The group doubled over in laughter. One kid had to sit down on the curb to laugh.

"Are you *urinating?*" Ben asked the boy. "Are you? You're *urinating,* aren't you?"

His audience was falling down in the grass, laughing. These kids didn't even live in our neighborhood. They were just following Ben home.

It was then that I first realized: My little brother is a rock star. An eight-year-old rock star. When did this happen?

I was only three years older, but already my humor had a musty old mothball quality to it. It was so heavy and obvious. *Here's the setup. And . . . here comes the punch line!* (*Ba da boom.*) I'd get a polite but weak *hahaha* laugh track.

Ben could just shrug his shoulders, extend his arms, and say, "And you know what happened then? *That guy* urinated, too!" And people would fall on the ground laughing.

The funny thing was, it *was* funny. But only Ben could pull it off. At the dinner table, Ben could slather his baked potato with butter, take a huge bite of it, and say, while chewing, "How's that working out for you, you old potato head?" And you couldn't *not* laugh at him.

Ben's third-grade class was studying the ancient Egyptians. At dinner, he told us the latest theories about how the pyramids were built.

"And *some* experts say they didn't use slaves at all, but created a vortex by chanting," he explained. "And *that's* how they lifted those stones so high."

"Fascinating," said Dad.

"Can we *please* talk about leaves?" Laura asked in her frantic little elf voice.

Laura's first-grade class was studying the seasons. Her assignment was to collect and identify ten beautiful fall leaves. She had until Halloween to do this, but she began worrying about the project the day it was assigned, pulling entire branches off trees and filling a black plastic trash bag with every leaf she could find between our house and the elementary school.

She agonized over the selection process, polling us individually and collectively.

"Okay, which do you think is prettier?" Laura asked as we ate dessert. With one hand she gently held up a huge, crisp yellow leaf. In the other hand she cradled a smaller but brilliant red leaf.

"The yellow one," said Ben, before biting confidently into a Bargain Bonanza oatmeal sandwich cookie.

"I'm with Ben," said Dad. "You can't beat a good yellow leaf."

"But look at the red one," said Clara, staring as if mesmerized. "It's *amaaaaaaaaaazing*."

"The red one *is* pretty," I agreed, trusting Clara's artistic judgment.

Mom dipped her cookie in a cup of tea. "They're both so pretty," she said. "Do you have to choose just one?"

Laura's enthusiasm was turning to panic.

"I have to pick ten leaves and I have *TWENTY THOUSAND MILLION* in here!" she said, throwing the bag of leaves on the floor and running from the table in tears.

Laura had it, too: Whatever this thing was that made easy stuff — leaf projects, school-supply shopping, true/false questions — difficult.

I remembered hating those leaf projects in first grade, too. Is that when it started?

Why do we have to pick just ten? Can't we bring in all the pretty leaves we find? Is there a shortage of leaves? Leaves are free! This is one thing I can do as well as anybody. Nobody can out-leaf me. Let's cover the whole room with leaves! Let's wallpaper the hall with leaves!

Mom picked up the trash bag and followed Laura to her room. Together they spent the next hour picking out the ten prettiest leaves.

Dad, Clara, Ben, and I cleared the table. Sally played alone under the dining room table. (That kid. She could entertain herself for hours just humming a little song to herself.) I wondered if Sally had the leaf problem, too. Too early to tell. Ben certainly didn't have it.

"They're just *leaves*," Ben said to Dad. "Why can't she just pick a leaf, any leaf? They're *all* pretty."

Clara and I loaded the dishwasher while Dad and Ben retreated to the living room. (*"And, Dad, you won't believe how they made mummies. What they did was . . ."*)

Clara spent that evening at the dining room table, working on the speech she had to give to the whole seventh-grade class the following Wednesday. I didn't know if she had the leaf disease or not. Clara understood it, but she certainly wasn't crippled by it like I was. Like Laura was.

Poor Laura. The things that scared her: Crossing guards. Ladybugs. Mrs. Flanagan, the children's librarian at the Normal Public Library.

Somehow Mom had not picked up on this last one because she asked Mrs. Flanagan to babysit for us on Saturday night so she and Dad could go to a Parents-As-Teachers potluck at the elementary school.

"Of course you guys don't *need* a babysitter," Mom explained when Clara and I protested that we were perfectly capable of taking care of ourselves. "But I thought it'd be a treat. Just think: Mrs. Flanagan works at the library. She'll know all the best bedtime stories."

That night Mrs. Flanagan told Ben and me the story of the Little Match Girl.

"Once there was a little girl whose job was selling matches," Mrs. Flanagan began, sitting in the rocking chair she'd asked me to carry to our room from my parents' bedroom.

"Matches?" Ben said, sitting up in bed. "That was her *real job?*"

"Shhhhhhhhhyes," Mrs. Flanagan said in her official story time voice. "She was very poor. And that was her job. Selling matches to people on the street. And one night, it was very, very cold. And no one was buying the Little Match Girl's matches."

Ben again: "Why wouldn't they buy her matches?"

"Just listen, Ben," I said from my bed.

"No one was buying her matches," Mrs. Flanagan continued. "And it was so cold. So the poor Little Match Girl lit a match."

Ben giggled.

"Yes, she lit a match," said Mrs. Flanagan, "which is a very dangerous thing to do."

"Not if you know how to do it, it's not," Ben said in a knowing voice to the wall.

"Ben, c'mon, just listen," I said.

"Well, when she lit a match," Mrs. Flanagan said, "the Little Match Girl looked in the flame and saw a little stove. And it was so pretty and warm. And then, poof! The flame went out. So she lit another match. This time the Little Match Girl looked in the flame and saw a table filled with hot food. And the Little Match Girl just stared at all the food because she had not had a meal in days. And then, poof! The flame went out."

Ben was snoring.

Good. Because this Little Match Girl's in trouble, I can feel it.

Mrs. Flanagan droned on: "And so the Little Match Girl lit another match. And this time she looked very closely in the flame and saw the face of her old dead grandmother, who said, 'Oh, you poor Little Match Girl. You're so cold and hungry. Come to me. I'll keep you warm.' And then, poof! The flame went out. And then the Little Match Girl lit all her matches. Because it was so cold. And the next day when they found the Little Match Girl, she was dead. And surrounding her stiff, frozen little body were the charred matches she'd lit in the final hours of her little life."

Silence.

She paused. "And so the moral of the story," said Mrs. Flanagan, "is never, ever play with matches."

"Because," she said darkly (*did she think we were idiots?*), "you could die."

You mean old woman. Why are you so mean to us?

"I think Ben's asleep," I said.

"Oh," Mrs. Flanagan said. "That's good."

Silence.

"Charles, dear, would you carry this rocker down to the girls' room so I can tell them a story?"

I crawled out of bed and did as told.

"Thank you, honey," she said in the hallway outside Laura and Clara's room. "Sleep tight."

"Okay," I said, turning back toward my room.

Wait. Say something.

"Um, Mrs. Flanagan?"

"Yes, dear?"

"Would you mind telling Clara and Laura another story? I'm pretty sure that Little Match Girl will give Laura nightmares."

"Oh, do you think so?"

"Yeah. I do. Something like *The Velveteen Rabbit* would be good. Laura really likes that one."

I turned and walked back to my room, already seeing the thousand flying, laughing, ice-covered fingers that would haunt my dreams for the next five nights I slept — or tried to sleep — in my bed.

11.

I thought of the Little Match Girl all during Mass on Sunday. Jesus seemed to have more in common with her than with God. But according to the Bible, Jesus was both God and man. Not God and Little Match Girl.

After Mass we had Sunday school in the kitchen of the rectory. Sister Theresa Paul asked us to draw a scene from the Bible that illustrated the divine Trinity.

"And we all remember what *Trinity* means," Sister Theresa Paul began. "God the Father, God the Son, and God the Holy Spirit. Three beings in one. So you'll draw three things, but it's really one."

This was the same woman who said during an art lesson, "And when you're drawing snow, remember to use a *blue* crayon."

I found this kind of reasoning maddening. But my brother, Ben, embraced these inconsistencies without hesitation.

"So it's like a s'more?" he asked. He was sitting on the kitchen counter.

"A *what?*" said Sister Theresa Paul, smiling an artificially sweet smile.

"S'more," continued Ben, unfazed. "You know, like when you're burning leaves and you roast a marshmallow on a stick and put it on a graham cracker. And then you put a little piece of chocolate on top. And then a graham cracker on top of that. And you smash it all together. It melts into one — what's the word — *Trinity?*"

Sister smiled again. She closed her dead fish eyes before responding.

"But Ben, the Holy Trinity is indivisible. You can't separate God the Father from Jesus or from the Holy Spirit."

"You can't separate the chocolate from the marshmallow from the graham cracker once they're all melted together," Ben said, not even trying to be a wise guy.

"Thank you, Ben."

"Oh, and you know what else?" Ben said, spearing his finger through the air. "You can make s'mores for an after-school snack. You just stick a marshmallow on a spoon and roast it over a burner on the stove."

"Thank you, Ben."

"But don't use a wooden spoon!"

My younger brother had an epiphany while I was trying to figure out how to illustrate "Jesus wept" with sixteen Crayola crayons.

But I couldn't draw. Not like Clara could. Her home-made posters hanging in the junior high didn't look nearly as bad as I'd feared.

There were now eight candidates running for seventh-grade president: four boys and four girls. Only one of the boys made campaign posters, and his were dull, black-and-white banners made on a dot matrix printer.

The girl candidates all had colorful signs created with fancy graphics software. (*If YOU believe in Seventh-Grade PRIDE, Vote LORI LYONS for President!*)

But Clara's handmade posters looked just as good, I thought. Better! Besides, didn't they show what a hard worker Clara was? How dedicated and imaginative she was? I hoped her classmates were picking up on the deeper meaning in all this. How could they miss it?

Was there a chance Clara could really pull this thing off? I was starting to believe it could happen. Then again, I was beginning to believe anything could happen after I finally (*finally!*) convinced Dad to buy my cello on a payment plan, rather than continue renting it another year.

"It's only eleven dollars more a week," I explained to Dad that Sunday night. "But at the end of the year, I can keep it."

"Let me see the contract," Dad said.

I knew he hated stuff like this, but it *did* make sense. He read the fine print, looking, I thought, for an excuse to say no.

"Clara's had her flute since third grade," I said. "And since I'm in junior high orchestra now, well —"

"Clara's flute cost about a *fifth* of what this thing costs," Dad said. "That's twenty percent, Charles."

Why was I so stupid? I was trying to play the fair card, but I'd played the stupid card instead. Why did I even try?

Of course I was the only one in orchestra who still rented my instrument. I was a Harrisong. We were renters! Who cared. I didn't even really like my stupid cello. It was so big and heavy. Felt like playing a dead horse. And that stupid RENTAL sticker taped on the case like some kind of scar. I even hated my white orchestra notebook. It was too white, too naked. It looked like a plucked chicken next to my other notebooks. Why did I even bother —

"Well, why not?" Dad was saying.

What?

"You've been playing that thing for a couple years now," he said. "You seem to like it. Tell you the truth, I wouldn't mind hearing some classy music around this place at night. Maybe when Ben and Laura get older, one of them could play the violin and the other the —"

Could this be true?

Dad was laughing.

"Yeah, we'll put Mom on drums. Sally on tambourine. I've got a guitar around here somewhere I used to —"

"Thank you!" I said, dazed.

I was going to *own* my cello? No more waiting around till everyone left orchestra practice so I could lock the stupid cello in the closet with the band uniforms? No more being the last one out of practice? And I didn't have to share it with any of my siblings? I felt light-headed with happiness.

"Thank you . . . just . . . so much!" I said.

And then I ran up to my room before Dad could see I was crying.

Later that night after taking a shower, I walked past Clara and Laura's room. Laura was sound asleep. Clara was working by a clamp light attached to her bed.

"What're you doing?" I whispered, standing in the doorway.

She held up a round piece of construction paper with a smiley face drawn in the center.

"More buttons," she said softly. "I'm *postered out.*"

I smiled.

"Dad's going to let me buy my cello," I said quietly.

"Cool!" she said, cutting an intricate pattern of curls into the paper.

"I know," I said. "About time."

I turned to continue to my room. Then I remembered the conversation I'd overheard between Mom and Dad.

"I can't believe I forgot to tell you this," I said, recalling with a chill the information I'd gleaned on the drive home from Mass. "Mom's thinking about coming to school on Wednesday to hear you give your campaign speech."

"I know," Clara whispered. "I invited her."

"You — ?"

"Yeah," said Clara. "I figured I might feel a little nervous before my speech. So I thought if I could look out in the audience and see Mom there, I'd feel better."

MIGHT feel a little nervous? So she invited MOM? Who were these people in my family?

"Right," I said. "Good idea."

Say something nice.

"Well," I stammered, slipping into my puppet voice. "I hope the speech goes great!"

"It will," Clara said softly. "Positive thinking!"

And like a cougar, Clara sprang silently from her bed. She flexed her muscles and bared her teeth like Ben and his friends did when they were imitating professional wrestlers.

She held her hand over her mouth and laughed noiselessly. I tried to do the same. But inside I prayed: *God, let her win. She has to win. Don't let her lose. If she loses, she'll die. I'll die. Make her win. This is easy for You. Please. Thank you.*

Amen.

12.

On Monday in Language Arts, Mrs. Johnson assigned our first book report of the year. I decided to do mine on *To Kill a Mockingbird*. After school, I rode my bike to the Normal Public Library and checked out the book.

I was back home in the kitchen, using a spatula to scrape the last traces of mint chocolate chip ice cream out of the carton, when Clara got home. She had an armload of new poster board, which she dumped on the kitchen table, next to my books.

"*To Kill a Mockingbird,*" she said. "Cool! Read it to me while I make posters, will you, Chums?"

"I thought you were postered out," I said, between bites of ice cream.

"I'm just making five more for the cafeteria," she said, grabbing a handful of Cowboy Cal's Country Crunch Flakes from the cupboard. She stuffed the cereal in her mouth, gathered up the poster board, and took the back stairs two by two up to her room. I followed her.

I sat on the floor, my back leaning against Laura's bed, while Clara stretched out on her bed, surrounded by art supplies. I read out loud while Clara made her final batch of posters, which said simply: FRIDAY IS ELECTION DAY! DON'T FORGET TO VOTE!

Clara stopped me periodically for clarification.

"Chums, you gotta read the characters with different voices so I can tell who's who."

So I did. Clara roared at my portrayal of Mrs. Dubose, the morphine addict, and Aunt Alexandra, Atticus's sister, who was not fat, but "solid," and whose "protective garments" pulled her bosom up to "giddy heights."

"Like Mrs. Flanagan!" Clara said, and she laughed for five minutes straight.

"Okay, keep reading," she finally said, waving her hand in front of her face. I tried to, but Clara burst out laughing again.

"Wait, stop," she cried. "I gotta get Mrs. Flanagan's giddy bosom out of my head."

I used the break to stand and stretch. I was surprised to see that, judging by the clock/radio on Clara's dresser, I'd been reading aloud for almost two hours. I was less surprised to see the five yardsticks of gum I'd given Laura for her birthday, still unopened and propped against the radiator.

I pulled out the banana gum yardstick and leaned on it, jauntily, with my feet crossed like the Planters Peanut man.

"Speaking of Mrs. Flanagan," I said.

Clara almost fell off her bed laughing.

"No, seriously," I said, uncrossing my feet. "Mrs. Flanagan saw me checking *To Kill a Mockingbird* out of the library. She said there's some mystery about who really wrote it."

"There's no *mystery*," said Clara. "Look at the cover. It says right there: Harper Lee."

"I know," I said, returning the banana gum to its rightful place next to the grape. "But Mrs. Flanagan says some people think Truman Capote was the real author."

"Who cares who wrote it?" Clara said. "I wouldn't even care if some of it's just made up. It's a great story."

I watched her shake gold glitter on a smiley face in the middle of the o in VOTE.

"Doesn't Atticus remind you of God?" I asked her.

"God God or Jesus God?" she said.

"God God."

"Hmmmm," Clara said. "If you mean someone who's completely good and kind, definitely Atticus. But like I've told you, I just don't think of God as being a regular old *man*."

I did. I envisioned God back in His Genesis days as Atticus, played by Gregory Peck. Strong. Wise. That shiny black hair and superhero square jaw. Now in His semi-retirement days at Bargain Bonanza, God was probably more like an old B-actor in those always disappointing made-for-television movies.

We had spaghetti for dinner that night. Afterward, Dad told everyone to "adjourn to the living room" so Clara could practice her campaign speech on us.

Her giggles gone, Clara delivered the speech. Her key points were that, as an oldest child, she was used to responsibility. She was also good at art projects and would try to convince the school administration to let her paint a mural — educational, if necessary — in the cafeteria.

But most importantly, she would encourage everyone to think positively.

"It's important to have a positive way of thinking," Clara said with the sweeping hand gestures I'd seen her practicing around the house. "Because WE can do great things. WE can be great people. WE can be the best seventh-grade class in the history of Normal Junior High."

She signaled for us to applaud. We did.

"But it all starts HERE," she said, pointing to her head, her index finger disappearing in her curls.

"Positive thinking!" she orated. "We must envision how GREAT we can be. And then we must match our ACTIONS to our thoughts. Our DEEDS to our words. Only THEN will we become the AWESOME seventh-grade class I KNOW we can be. Thank you. And have a GREAT year!"

My parents jumped to their feet and applauded thunderously.

Why were they building her up like this? Sure, it was a good speech. And Clara was the best candidate, no doubt. But they were giving her false hopes.

I smiled and clapped with as much enthusiasm as I could muster. The truth was, I felt extremely conflicted about all this. Part of me was almost bursting with pride. *My sister —* giving a speech in the school auditorium in front of the entire *seventh grade? My sister —* president of her *class?!* Then again, if she lost, could there be a worse humiliation — for her and me both? (*My sister — a loser?*)

It was almost ten o'clock when I stopped in her doorway on my way back from brushing my teeth. Clara was sitting on the floor, clipping her toenails.

"Great speech," I said.

"Thanks, Chums," Clara said, not looking up from her feet. "I feel weirdly good about all this."

"Yeah," I said.

I watched her struggle with a rascally nail on her big toe. She looked up at me and smiled.

"What, Chums?"

"Nothing," I said. "Just . . . um . . . do you feel at all *anxious* about the election?"

I hoped she knew what *anxious* meant. I'd learned myself only that day when Mrs. Stephens, a counselor from Normal Elementary, had cornered me in the hall, on my way to the restroom.

"Charles Harrisong!" she said. "You're just the person I'm looking for."

What? Why was my elementary school counselor here? Why was she looking for me?

We stood next to the water fountain, across from the doors to the cafeteria. The smell of boiled hot dogs and green beans filled the hallway.

"Charles," she said.

"Yes, ma'am."

"Charles."

Oh, no. What was it? Has somebody died? Was it Dad? Mom? Was our house on fire? What? Oh, God. Someone has kidnapped Sally. Just tell me and get it over with!

"I wanted to know how you're feeling."

How I'm feeling?! It was nothing. Oh! Thank you, God.

"I feel fine," I said, relieved.

"Are you liking junior high?"

"Yeah," I lied. "I like it . . . just fine."

"Charles, are you feeling anxious about anything?" she prodded.

What was she talking about?

"Well," I started. And then I stopped.

Wait. Relax! It's nothing. Don't let your voice slip into weird puppet mode.

"I'm anxious about . . . um, Halloween, I guess," I said. I looked around to make sure no one saw I was talking to a counselor.

I can't believe I'm talking to a counselor! If she brings up The Yearling, *I'll die.*

"I'm sorry," Mrs. Stephens said. "I'm not making myself clear. By *anxious,* I mean are you feeling any *anxiety.*"

She was making a strange face: half-smile, half-frown.

"Are you worried about anything?" she pressed.

"Worried?" I said, laughing. *Conversation with Mrs. Stephens* raced to the coveted number one slot on my *Things to Worry About* list.

"No!" I said.

All wrong. Sound casual. This is nothing. Keep it light! She probably doesn't even remember it. The Yearling *incident. Me sitting in her office. "It certainly is a sad book, Charles. I cried when I read it, too. If you don't want to finish it, you don't have to. There are lots of books in the library. You can pick a different book."*

"I mean, sure," I said, shrugging my shoulders. "I worry about tests and grades and stuff. But it's not *anxiety.*"

I said the word *anxiety* like it was a disease. Like it was *leprosy.* I shrugged again and scrunched up my face like a happy puppet. Like I did in her office that day last year. (*"I think it's just my allergies. I have hay fever. Ragweed and stuff like that."*)

"Your grades are fine, Charles," she said. "You know that. But if you ever want to talk, I'm here. Okay? On Mondays and Wednesdays."

She gave me a significant look. (*"Of course those things really happened, Charles. If they hadn't killed the deer, that poor family would've died of starvation."*)

"Sure," I said. "Right! If I ever want to talk."

"About anything."

"Okay. Thanks."

I flew back to class. My bladder could wait.

If I ever wanted to talk? To my elementary school counselor?! Oh, sure. Right after I take off all my clothes, dip my body in purple paint, and run through the school naked. Was she crazy?

No, wait. Oh, my gosh. Did she think I was crazy? Was that what this was about? Was she asking everyone this? Or just me? Why was she following me to junior high? Was she tracking me?

Clara was saying something about the election. One conversation at a time, I reminded myself.

"So if I win, I win," she was saying, folding her nail clippers into a black leatherette case. "And if I don't, I don't. No big deal. I'll have more time to do other things, like start a coed synchronized swim club. Wouldn't that be *so* cool, Chums? I could make up swimming routines, and then we could put on water shows in the summer for all the parents. And I want to try out for the school play, too. I think they're doing *Kiss Me, Kate* this year."

Coed synchronized swim club? Kiss Me, Kate?!

Clara's Election and Conversation with Mrs. Stephens were now tied for number one on my *Things to Worry About* list. I would have to worry about coed synchronized swimming and school plays later.

13.

I couldn't sleep on Monday night, so I took my pillow into the bathroom and continued reading *To Kill a Mockingbird*. I read it again on Tuesday during study hall and probably would've finished it that night. But Clara wanted me to start reading to her from where we left off Monday.

"C'mon, Chums," she said after dinner. "I need something to relax me so I don't get the jitters about my speech tomorrow."

She was back at work on the bunny mural. She had spent the afternoon painting the Heroes of the Civil Rights Movement (Dr. Martin Luther King, Jr., Rosa Parks, Atticus Finch) as rabbits. She was now kneeling on Laura's bed and painting Vincent van Gogh as a one-eared rabbit.

I sat on the floor and read for close to an hour while Laura had her bath and the sound of the vacuum cleaner droned downstairs. When my eyes grew tired from reading, I closed the book, leaned back on my elbows, and watched Clara paint.

"You're going to be a famous artist," I told her.

"You really think so?" she asked. "I would *love* that! To be able to paint all day? That would be heaven. What about you? What are you going to be?"

I hadn't a clue.

"You know what I can see you as?" Clara said. "A writer."

A writer? Me?

"You're a really good writer," she said, dunking her paintbrush in the Miracle Whip jar and swirling it through the mouse-colored water.

"Me?"

"Yes! Remember those letters you wrote home from Boy Scout camp? Mom and I fought over who got to read them first."

What?! Really?

"And then at dinner, Dad read the letters out loud, and we all laughed again. They were hilarious. Chums, don't you remember those funny letters you wrote us from camp?"

Of course I remembered. I'd spent hours writing them, trying to sound like the light and breezy camper I wasn't. *The food here is edible, unless you're one of those demanding Scouts like me who prefers to live for a while — like until dessert.*

But Dad read my letters at dinner? They *laughed?*

"You could be a writer like Harper Lee," Clara said.

"Or Truman Capote," I countered.

The more I thought about that literary hijinx, the angrier I got. I'd spent my lunch hour writing a letter to the publisher:

Dear Sir or Madam,
     Can you please tell me who the real author of To Kill a Mockingbird is? If it's Truman Capote, that's fine. I have no plans to sue you for fraud. I'd just like to know the truth.
     Also, can you tell me if the story is true or made up? If it's a combination of both, can you tell me (approximately) how much is real and how much is made up?
Thank you,
Charles ("Charlie") Harrisong

I found the name and address of the publisher in the front of the book. I used my milk money to buy a stamp from the office. The secretary let me buy an envelope for a nickel. (*Lookit, if I give you one for free, the whole sixth-grade class is gonna want envelopes, and somebody has to pay for this stuff.*)

I should've typed the letter, I thought, as I watched Clara stand on the bed and paint spiky red rabbit hair on van Gogh's head.

"And no, I don't think writers are weirder than other people," Clara was saying. "It's just that a lot of writers write about the weirdness that's part of normal life. I can see you being one of those really cool writers who lives in New York City and wears tweed jackets with elbow patches. You'd go out for coffee in the morning with your notebook. And you'd see people at the café and you'd know their stories just by looking at them. That's what you'd write about."

"And what if I saw you at the café?" I asked. "What would I write about you?"

"Well," she said, turning from the mural and fluffing her brown scribble of curls dramatically. "Of course you'd start off by describing my physical beauty. My glooooorious hair. My finely chiseled features. How I look like a painting by . . . um . . . er . . . oh, shoot. Now I can't think of any famous lady painters."

"A painting by the world-famous artist Clara Harrisong," I said, following her lead. "Clara Harrisong, the young artist from the heartland whose Manhattan gallery has become the favorite of the New York jet set. Harrisong herself cuts quite a figure with her Renaissance hair and alabaster skin."

Clara jumped on the bed.

"*SEE?* This is what I mean! You're going to be a writer! I just *KNOW* it. I know it, I know it, I know it!"

God, how she believed in me. Nobody believed in me like Clara.

But my sister was hardly a reliable judge. She'd also told me that I was the funniest person in Normal once when we were riding bikes to Dairy Queen and I'd said: "Cross your fingers the deaf girl is working!" She never was. I told Clara it was crazy to think we'd luck out again and get a second Peanut Buster Parfait by mistake from the counter girl who couldn't hear. But Clara just hoped without thinking.

14.

Effective Wednesday morning, I no longer rented my cello; I rented-to-*own* it. By Wednesday afternoon, I was cursing my cello. Specifically, the *my-ness* of it. I wanted to dis-own it.

Every Wednesday now for the rest of my life, I would be forced to strap the cello in its case and carry the thing — big as that dang rocking chair — from the band room in the school basement, up the stairs, and then two blocks home.

I longed for those carefree rental days of fourth and fifth grade when I could dump the stupid cello in the band closet and be done with it. I was still the last one out of orchestra practice. The only difference now was that it was because I was a beast of burden.

On the day of Clara's speech, I loitered in the band room after practice — tying my shoes, retying them, zipping my backpack, unzipping it — so no one would see my clumsy dance with the cello up the stairs.

I was eager — and *anxious* — to hear how the speech had gone. But I can't say I was hurrying to get home. The fact is — and I do admit it — I was dawdling, as I often did after the last bell rang.

Though I endured rather than enjoyed school, of all the long hours in the school day, the after-school limbo was my favorite. The halls emptied quickly of students and chaos. It went from airport terminal loud to funeral parlor quiet in minutes. Plus, there was that happy feeling of another day behind you. One more square to X off the calendar. I thought of the slaves who built pyramids. Never mind Ben's theory about stones dancing in a vortex of chanting. It wasn't that complicated. People like me built those pyramids.

There had always been and would always be people like me who carried stuff — boulders, cellos, other people's mattresses — on our backs and up endless flights of stairs. We were the blessed and the meek. But, according to the Bible, we would inherit the earth! I would be the boy hero of heaven. Maybe I'd meet Ponce de León.

"Need any help with that monster?"

It was Mr. Peterson. The band director. He was pointing a violin bow at my cello.

"No, I'm fine," I said, looking up like a tortoise from under my cello shell. "Thanks, anyway."

"Okay!" he said. And he passed me on the stairs, his Hush Puppies mimicking the sound of his metronome.

"Charlie," he said, stopping at the landing and turning around.

"Yes, sir?"

"Everything okay in your world?" he asked, looking at me and stroking his bow. He was scrunching his lips and his eyebrows and making that weird happy sad face that Mrs. Stephens had made.

Why was everyone asking me this? Was this a trick question? A trap? No. This is nothing.

"Everything's fine!" I said in my cheeriest voice.

"Because if you ever want to talk or anything, you know I'm all ears."

Now Mr. Peterson? What the —?

"Right," I said. "Thanks!"

"Okay, then." And he turned and continued up the stairs.

I could feel Conversation with Mr. Peterson sneaking onto my *Worry* list. I tried to block it.

Mr. Peterson is a complete goof! I mean, he seems like a nice enough guy. He tries really hard to make orchestra halfway decent. But he's a dork! Those cheesy houndstooth check jackets he wears? And this bit about being all ears. ALL EARS? Now there's a mental image!

I imagined Mr. Peterson's face morphing into a gigantic ear. *Haw!* This was better. Maybe I could learn to talk myself out of these things. Plus, the stupid cello was so freaking heavy, I simply could not worry about Mr. Peterson and carry the thing at the same time.

I reached the top of the stairs. Now to my locker. And then home. Just two short blocks.

It was 3:30. The halls were empty. I liked it like this. Less chance of a confrontation with a classmate. Or another teacher.

I got to my locker and opened the combination lock: 14. 24. 28. I ran through my Wednesday class schedule, trying to remember what homework I had: Social Studies, Math, Science . . .

From the end of the hall, I heard the glass double doors to the outside open. Some kids were spilling through the doorway. They were running toward me.

It's okay. Just get the books you need and go.

I started the rundown again in my head: Social Studies. Math. Science. Language Arts.

"Shut up!" I heard one of the kids saying.

"No, you shut up!"

But they weren't fighting. They were laughing and telling one another to shut up. This is what kids did. They didn't want to join a synchronized swim club and put on shows for their parents. I kept my eyes fixed on the interior of my locker.

"Seventh grade RULES!" one of the girls said. Someone

did something in response. I couldn't make out what it was. Physical comedy. They all laughed.

They were doing something else now. I heard the sounds of cardboard ripping. I looked in their direction. They were boys and girls from my class. No, they were in Clara's class. No, wait. Some of each. Six, seven. Two more. Nine of them.

They were running. They were stopping and looking at something on the walls. Then they were laughing. Then they were running again.

What are they doing?

They were coming my way.

What do they want?

Now I could see. They were tearing posters. They were laughing and ripping campaign posters in half.

One girl had a marker. She and a boy were writing on the posters.

"Hey, it's Charlie Harrisong!" the girl said.

She was pointing at me, but her hips were pivoted, like a cheerleader, so she could be admired from multiple views.

I saw the purse slung diagonally across her chest. I remembered then. Taylor. One of the popular girls from that day at Bargain Bonanza.

"Harrisong?" I heard a boy say.

"Yeah, that's her brother."

I stopped breathing. *Her? They knew Clara? What were they going to say about her? Whatever it is, don't listen to it. Just tune it out. Think of something else. You're not here. They're not real.*

I faced my locker and blindly shuffled my books. Out of the corner of my eye I could see Taylor writing something on a poster while the boy (*Wasn't he a seventh grader?*) looked on and laughed.

Now I recognized the boy. Randy Breedlove. Son of Mr. Breedlove, the district scoutmaster. Randy had been christened alpha male clique leader of Normal Junior High based on the breathless rumors that he had gotten an eighth-grade girl pregnant over the summer. (So *that's* why all the Scouts were laughing in the camp photo.)

Randy grabbed the marker from Taylor. He looked at me and wrote something on the poster. Taylor put her hand over her mouth.

"Oh, now that's *mean!*" she said.

Well, of course it's mean. He's writing on somebody's sign.

And then they both screamed with laughter. Taylor was so pretty. How could she be so mean? And why was mean funny?

The other kids were running out the double doors. Taylor and Randy lagged behind, scribbling on some posters, ripping others, and laughing (*HAHAHAHAHAHA!*) as they ran. So athletic in their meanness! So merit-badge worthy.

Now Taylor was standing at the door, whispering something to Randy. He was laughing. They were looking at me.

Oh, God. Keep going. Just go.

"Hey, Harrisong."

It was Randy. He was holding the door open for Taylor (*Such the gentleman!*). As she leaped through the door, he swatted her bottom playfully (*Such the player!*). Still watching her, he yelled over his shoulder to me:

"The deer dies."

The doors slammed shut. They were gone. The hallway was quiet.

I closed my locker. Forget homework. Just get home.

I picked up my cello and started walking down the hall, toward the double doors. Toward home. And then I saw it.

One of Clara's posters. They'd crossed out all of POSITIVE WAY OF THINKING except for the first letters: P, W, and T. Under these they'd written, vertically, in sloppy second-grade letters: OOR HITE RASH.

Oh, I get it. *Poor White Trash.*

I leaned my cello against a locker and pulled the poster board off the wall. I ripped it in half. And then in fourths.

But there was another one next to it. They'd written the same thing: POOR WHITE TRASH.

Why had Clara made so many stupid posters?

I told her this'd never work. Or I tried to, anyway. I should've told her that very first night at dinner when she brought up the idea of running for president.

I ripped the second poster down. And then in half. And then —

The double doors opened again. It was Clara. Sally was with her.

"Chumsley!" Clara yelled. "Mom's here."

What? No. This isn't possible.

"Look, Charles!" said Sally. She was cradling something in her arms. "Laura and me got rabbits. Mine's Mr. Fluff. Hers is Mrs. Fluff."

"Mom thought you might need help carrying your cello home," Clara said. "She said to hurry. She's got groceries. Ice cream."

What? Mom was giving me a ride home? Why? She'd never done this before.

"C'mon!" said Clara. She was chewing gum. "Mint chocolate chip."

She was standing inside the double doors now, using her back to prop one door open.

Her eyes dropped. She saw the ripped poster board in my hands. Her gum-chewing jaws froze.

"Charles! Are those *my* posters? What are you doing to my posters?

NO! This isn't happening. This isn't happening. This isn't happening.

Clara was walking toward me, saying something. Her face looked distorted, as if her nose were melting to make room for her swelling eyes and mouth. For a split second she looked like an alien. I stared down at my hands.

"I cannot *BELIEVE* you, Charles," Clara said, enunciating every syllable. "What in the world would make you do something like this?"

Oh, this is better. Let her think I did it. Let her think I'm jealous. Good idea, God! Thank You for paying attention. You're good when You want to be! Ha! Yes, You are!

I started ripping the posters into smaller and smaller pieces. Faster and faster.

She'll never be able to put these back together.

I glanced up. Clara was still walking toward me, her arms hung loosely at her sides like a rag doll. I refocused my eyes on my fluttering hands.

"And when I tell DAD about this," Clara said.

God, she was mad.

"Is Charles going to get in trouble?"

It was Sally.

"You BET he's going to get in trouble!" said Clara. "BIG trouble. Charles, you KNOW how much time I spent making —"

She stopped walking, dead in her tracks.

Now what?

I looked up from my hands. Clara was looking at a bulletin board.

The bulletin board! I hadn't even looked there.

I had missed one. Clara and I read it at the same time.

Written in big black letters under CLARA HARRISONG FOR 7TH-GRADE CLASS PRESIDENT were the words: UGLY BITCH.

15.

Clara read the words and said in a thin, airy voice: "I'm . . . I'm going home now."

Then she turned around, bumped into Sally (*"Oh. Gosh."*), and ran out the double doors.

Sally's new rabbit was suddenly shooting like a cannonball down the hallway. Sally was yelling at me to catch him. Somehow I did. I'm not sure how.

The whole time I was trying to catch that rabbit (*Was it five minutes? Ten? An hour?*), I was hissing under my breath, "GOD, I hate this place! GOD, I hate all these MEAN, STUPID people!"

That made Sally cry.

"Don't *say* that, Charles!"

I snapped at her: "Would you just be quiet? Just BE quiet! Would you just stand there and BE QUIET while I catch your STUPID rabbit?"

She only cried louder. And then I knocked my cello over, and it hit the floor hard. I heard the crack inside me.

I don't know how I got home that day. Did I walk, or get

a ride with Mom? I know somebody told Mom and Dad about the posters. It wasn't me.

I know we didn't eat dinner that night until late. And when we did, it was a bucket of take-out chicken.

I remember that because I remember hearing Dad leave the house with Ben while Mom yelled, "Frank, don't! Please don't! Leave Ben here."

He's going to kill them, I thought. *Dad's going to find out who did it. And then he's going to kill them. With his bare hands. Dad's going to kill them. And Ben's going to help.*

I remember how loud Dad slammed the door on his truck (*THHHAWUMP*). He was mad. And he never got mad.

This was not my fault, I told myself as I sat in my bedroom, looking at Ben's plastic action figures strewn all over the floor. But if I hadn't been in that hallway, they might not have written what they wrote. Maybe I reminded them. Maybe I inspired them.

No, I didn't. They would've written it, anyway. But then a teacher or a custodian would've seen the posters and taken them down in the morning.

The only reason Clara saw the poster on the bulletin board was because I was still there. The only reason I was still there was because I was so slow leaving orchestra.

Because I had to own that stupid cello.

So it *was* my fault. But I was trying to help, wasn't I? Didn't that count for anything?

Actually, it was Mom's fault. Why did she have to encourage Clara to run for president when there was no chance on earth of her winning? And how many times did I have to tell Mom I did *not* want a ride?

No, it wasn't Mom's fault.

It was Dad's fault for making me buy that stupid cello.

No, it wasn't.

But now he's going to kill somebody, I thought. *Dad's going to kill somebody. And then he's going to go to jail. And I'll go to jail, too, because it's really my fault.*

Ten minutes later, I heard the familiar *thwump, thwump.* The sound of the truck doors slamming.

Dad was back! And Ben, too.

Oh, thank God he didn't kill anybody. We weren't going to jail.

"Charles!"

Mom was yelling up the stairs to me.

"Come get some chicken."

It was the teachers' fault, I thought, back in my room, pulling a piece of greasy chicken skin off a drumstick I couldn't eat. They had to know about these cliques. So why didn't they just *ban* them like they banned weapons and gum? Kick the clique leaders out of school. Send them to a military academy. Or at least to Catholic school.

It was God's fault. He just wasn't trying. He wasn't paying attention up in His secret office in the Bargain Bonanza ceiling. Couldn't He see what was going on down here? Were we hidden from His view by the cosmic Bargain Bonanza hay bales?

Of course He could see us. He was God!

But if He couldn't prevent stuff like this, then He wasn't a very good God. And if He *could* prevent stuff like this and chose *not* to, then He wasn't very nice. To let something like this happen to Clara?

Clara!

I felt limp with awfulness for her. How could someone call Clara such a terrible name? She was the kindest person I knew. Was she ugly? I didn't think so. She was Clara. She looked like a sister was supposed to look.

Maybe she wasn't the prettiest girl in her class. Was that such a crime? She had spent the past three weeks making posters — by hand. She had made buttons! She was willing to teach those idiots synchronized swimming routines.

And for this they defile her posters?

It didn't make sense. She was no threat to them. And didn't that word mean a female dog? Was that what they thought Clara was — *a dog?*

I thought of that stupid movie about the extraterrestrial dogs. All the dogs who took over Washington were male.

The cats were all female. No, wait. There was one girl dog. She was a singer in a cocktail lounge. She wore a long red dress with a diamond-studded dog collar and slinked around on top of a piano.

Is *that* the kind of dog they thought Clara was? Or were they just using that word because they knew it was hurtful?

These are not deep thinkers, I told myself. *Don't look for hidden meanings in the things they say and do. These are mean, stupid people.*

But why was I thinking about that movie again? I hated my brain for remembering garbage like this. I hated my mind's dogged (*Ack!*) insistence on hounding (*ugh*) me this way.

And thank you, Randy Breedlove, but I knew the deer died. I finished *The Yearling.* I didn't want to pick a different book. I wanted to pick a different ending for *that* book.

Clara was still in her bedroom, alone. The door was closed.

Mom had been in there with her first. Then Dad came home and went in. Then Mom. Now Dad had fixed a plate of chicken for her.

Earlier that night the scene downstairs had been bad-TV awful. Laura's feelings were hurt that Clara had locked the door.

"It's my room, too!" Laura had sobbed in the kitchen to Mom. "And I *told* Clara I'd scratch her back and give her lit-tle arm tickles like she likes. And I don't *like* these Christmas cards. I know what 'peculiar' means. It means *odd*. You're making fun of us."

I could barely hear Mom answering her. Something about "not making fun" and "just a joke" and "don't have to send them."

Ben had his own questions.

"Well, I *know* we're white. But are we poor?"

How could Ben not know we were poor? I knew at his age. No one told me, but I knew it. I also knew there was no chance we would ever be rich. I knew it in the same way I knew we would never go to Paris for dinner.

Now it was almost ten o'clock. I was in bed, awake. Ben was sleeping. "I guess we'll just skip the Great Explorer stories tonight — right, Charles?" he'd said before falling asleep.

Oh, God. Don't let his world fall apart, too. He's The Funny Kid! He could BE Normal. Run away, Ben. Get out of here while you can. Go be a rock star somewhere.

I could hear Mom's and Dad's voices in Clara's room. Something about the election. Something something something "doesn't matter."

And then Clara's voice. She wasn't crying anymore. That was good.

"They're not very nice to him."

My heart stopped.

"It's because he's shy," Dad was saying.

"Not shy."

It was Clara again.

"That's what made him shy. . . . Didn't used to be like this. . . ."

Oh, God. Make it stop.

"If they'd just be nice to him . . . doesn't talk to anybody at school . . . always so nervous . . . alone in the cafeteria . . ."

I wanted to leave. I wanted to die.

It was true. I hated school. But I hated this more. I lay there, still as a corpse, staring at the ceiling.

I recited my silent prayer: *God, please let us be a normal family. Let us get a normal car. Let us live in a normal house and do normal things and not always be so embarrassing and different and loud. This is all I want. Please. Thank you.*

Amen.

Then I considered my options. I could kill myself.

Yeah, right. I couldn't even pull a Band-Aid off myself.

I could run away. I should run away. Maybe that's what they've been hoping for. Maybe that's why they did all those things that drove me crazy — to try to drive me away.

Clara was talking again.

"Sometimes he cries at school."

What?! I wasn't crying. My eyes watered sometimes, but I wasn't crying. It's just my hay fever.

"I don't know why. I guess he's sad."

It only happens when I think of things. People. That poor Little Match Girl. The stupid little deer who kept eating the family's crops.

Then my heart fell as if I'd been pushed from the high dive. It was suddenly so obvious. All this time I thought my family was pulling me down. But it was just the opposite. I was pulling *them* down. I was preventing *them* from *BEING* Normal.

Was that it?

It was.

God, why was I so dense? All those lists running through my head. I had it all wrong. *Embarrassing Things My Family Did* was really *Embarrassing Things I Did*. I was their secret shame. Their stupid little yearling.

A wave of shame crashed over me. I couldn't breathe. I was drowning.

And boys, lemme tell you something. If you don't know what you're doing, a drowning person can drown YOU. They pull you down with them.

I'd learned that much from Mr. Breedlove. And now I was the dummy pulling them down with me.

The door to Laura and Clara's room closed. I heard footsteps coming my way.

". . . think we should talk with him about it tonight." Dad.

"Not if he's sleeping. Let him sleep. We'll talk to him to-morrow." Mom.

I slammed my eyes shut.

God. Somebody. Please help me. I need a miracle. I'm begging You. Help me. Please. Thank You. Amen.

I said it once. Then I said it again. I repeated the prayer all night long.

But in the morning it was no better. I could not get out of bed. I could not go back to that school.

16.

Clara didn't go to school the next morning, either.

We both stayed in our rooms most of the day. I saw her at about noon, walking past my door with a bowl of cereal.

She peeked her head in my room.

"Hey," she said. She looked awful. Her eyes were somehow both puffy and hollowed out.

"Hey!" I said, tucking a haunted house mystery under the covers.

And that was it.

Mom checked in on me every hour or so. She was running errands all day.

"I'm going to the bank. Back in fifteen minutes. Want me to pick up a milk shake for you?"

"No, thanks."

An hour later: "I'm going to Bargain Bonanza. Need anything?"

"No. Thanks."

The phone rang a lot. Or what I thought was a lot for a Thursday, anyway. I tried to listen. Were these teachers calling?

The principal? Mrs. Stephens? It was impossible to decode the conversations from Mom's cryptic end.

"I think we should do it," Mom said at one point. "It's the right thing to do."

Are they sending me to boarding school? No, that's really expensive. Boot camp? A psychologist?

Another telephone conversation.

"Then just *keep* the deposit," Mom said. "If it's that important to you, just *keep* it."

At four o'clock that afternoon, Dad came home. He and Mom called a family meeting. (*Oh, God. Anything but family meetings.*) This was serious.

We gathered around the dining room table, where Laura and Sally had been making construction paper hats for their rabbits. Clara came downstairs. She was still wearing her nightgown. Her hair was dented on one side.

"Mom and I have made some decisions," Dad began. He looked at Mom and paused — *Do you want to jump in here? Okay, then I'll keep going.*

"It's almost four-thirty now," Dad continued. "We're going to spend the next, let's say three or four hours, packing our things. Then —"

"What things?" Ben interrupted. He was using two fingers to drive a tiny Hot Wheels car lazily up his arm.

"Just listen, Ben," Mom said.

Dad continued: "Everything you want to take with us —"

Ben again, to his arm: "Take with us where?"

"Ben, *listen!*" said Mom firmly, and she seized the car from his hand.

"We're leaving," Dad said.

And then he said the next part very quickly.

"We're going to leave tonight and drive to Alabama (*Alabama?*). It'll take us all night and most of tomorrow. When we get to Alabama, there'll be a boat waiting for us (*A boat?*). It might need a little fixing up. But I'm taking my tools. And Mom bought a new tent today (*A tent!*) at Bargain Bonanza (*Oh*). And we'll take our camping stuff and water and food. So."

Dad took a breath.

"What we need to do now is pack up," he said. "Ben, you know where the suitcases are in the attic. I think there are seven of 'em up there. Bring those down so we can start packing."

Ben leaped from his chair.

"Just a second, pal," Dad said. "We're still talking."

Ben repositioned himself — knees bent, hands resting on his thighs, lips pursed, eyes squinted in concentration — like a quarterback, waiting on the game play.

The sound from the TV in the living room flooded in to fill the heavy silence: "Roundin' up bargains, drivin' down prices, woo hoo woo hoo, it's all for YOU!" Sally dropped to the floor and began slithering on her belly toward the commercial.

"Now, we can't take everything with us," Dad said, scooping Sally up with one arm and dropping her on his knee. "I'd like to take as little as possible. I've got boxes in the back of my truck. Charles, can you get those after we're finished here? Anything we're not taking with us we'll put in boxes. I'll drop them off at the crisis shelter before we leave. We'll have to throw a lot of stuff away, too. I'll set the trash cans by the back door."

"We'll need lots of good rags for working on the boat," Mom said. "So anything that's not good enough for the shelter, put in a trash bag."

Mom put a box of black trash bags on the table. Laura's leaf bags.

"We're going on *vacation?*" asked Laura, scrunching her nose.

"Not vacation, honey," Dad said. "We're leaving. Moving."

"Where?" Laura asked, stretching the word out to two syllables. *Wear-er.*

"We've got some options," Dad said. "But we've got to get on the road tonight if we want that boat."

"What about school?" Clara asked. "I have a report on the Underground Railroad due Monday."

I didn't mention my book report. I remembered the library copy of *To Kill a Mockingbird* in my locker at school. The cracked cello in the hall. Clara's election on Friday.

"I have a spelling test *tomorrow!*" Ben said, slapping his forehead with both hands.

"Spelling tests, *schmelling* tests," Dad said, waving a hand in front of his face as if batting away a fly.

Clara and I looked at each other. *Was Dad drunk?*

"We're going to try doing school in a different way," Mom explained.

"Like homeschooling?" asked Laura.

"Yeah," Dad said. "Kind of like that. Okay?"

Wait! I wanted to say. *Not okay. Let's think about this! We don't have to do this on my account. I can fix this. Whatever it is. I'll pull out of it. Let's not do something crazy here.*

"This is something I've wanted to do for a long time," Dad said. "We need a change. Change is good."

Not always. Sometimes change is bad. Really bad. Let's just stop and think about this for a minute. Let me think. I need to make a list of all the things that could go wro —

"All right, then," Dad was saying. "Your first assignment is packing."

And we all went to our rooms and started packing. Like it was the most normal thing in the world.

Dad spent the next hour at the neighbors' house, trading his truck for a wooden trailer the station wagon could pull.

I heard Laura yell downstairs to Mom: "Mom! Can I take my birthday gum? I never finished all my gum."

So she *had* liked the gum. She just hadn't gotten around to chewing it.

"Yes, you may pack your gum," Mom answered. "But we're not taking everything with us. If you don't absolutely need it or use it every day, don't pack it. Clara will help you decide what to take. Won't you, honey?"

Don't ask Clara to do anything hard. Don't make her —

Then, thinly, from the girls' room: "Yes."

Oh, good. Clara's helping. That's good.

I debated whether to pack my school notebooks. All that clean paper. All those stupid people.

I started tearing out the pages I'd written on, thinking I'd save the rest. But soon I was ripping the stiff covers and bending the metal spirals and stuffing it all in a trash bag, along with the Boy Scout camp troop photo I found lurking in the bottom of my suitcase.

Ben got in the spirit of things.

"Hey! Anybody want my Little League trophies? If not, I'm thrrrrrrrrOOOWIN' 'em away."

The kid was enjoying this. Well, of course he was.

"When you can clean your closet at night," Ben told me, "it's not that bad. Not that bad at all."

At eight o'clock, Mom called us downstairs for dinner.

"Smorgasbord night," she said. And I saw the familiar single servings of reheated spaghetti, canned plums, fried chicken, dinner rolls. It was the once-a-month meal Clara and I always called Clean-Out-the-Refrigerator Night.

Sally was at the table, eating a piece of cold chicken. Dad was sitting on the kitchen floor. He had his big toolbox open and was filling it with supplies from under the sink.

"Charles and Ben," Mom said. "Sit down and eat while it's hot. Please."

I ate leftover spaghetti from a chipped cereal bowl. Ben was using a yellow dinner roll from the fried chicken place to clean out a jar of Bargain Bonanza strawberry jam.

"Were we kicked out of school or something?" Ben asked.

"Nobody was kicked out of school," Mom said.

"Dang it," Ben said, and he stuck the whole roll in his mouth.

Laura came clomping angrily down the stairs. Clara was behind her, saying something.

"That was just my practice one. I'll paint you another mural."

Laura was crying: "It will *never* be better than that one."

"Sure, it will," Clara said. "Because now I know how to do it. And you know the magician rabbit?"

"Yeah."

"I've been thinking," Clara said softly. "Next time we'll paint him the same way: a magician rabbit pulling a rabbit out of a hat. But *that* rabbit — the one in the hat — will be pulling a rabbit out of a hat, too. And the rabbit he's pulling out of a hat is *also* pulling a rabbit out of a hat. And it just keeps going like that."

"I don't (*sniff*) get it," Laura said.

"I'll show you what I mean," Clara said. "I'll sketch it for you later. It'll be really cool."

Clara was talking about painting. Thank you, God.

This, I thought, was truly a night to remember. And then I flinched at the freakish impossibility of *that* despised phrase popping up in my head, like a jeering jack-in-the-box in my brain.

I later learned — around the same time I learned about the yellow bricks — the word for the real-but-unreal-feeling world we were living in that night: *surreal.*

*   *   *

The rest of the night is a blur. Dad made three trips to the crisis shelter with boxes of our discards. Mom washed the inside of the refrigerator with bleach. She pulled the slipcovers off the living room furniture and balled the fabric up in a trash bag. Then she wrote and taped notes to the sofa, dining room set, and all of our beds: "Please do not throw away. Someone from St. Jude's will pick up."

We were packed by ten o'clock, but then spent another hour paring down.

"Come on, guys, we can't take all this," Dad said, looking at our heap of stuff piled next to the small trailer.

We had the car repacked by eleven-thirty. It took Mom another half hour to go through the house one last time, inspecting closets and bedrooms. (*And you wanted to know where those three cavities came from, young man?* she asked Ben. *I'd say those candy wrappers under your bed might have something to do with it.*)

Our house no longer looked scary. Just dingy and sad, like a broken old toy. I couldn't stay in those naked rooms. I sat in the car instead and waited.

It was after midnight when we finally pulled out of the driveway. We sat in our usual formation: Sally in the front, snuggled between Dad at the wheel and Mom with the map. Clara and I sat in the backseat with Laura between us, asleep. Ben was in the way back.

We were past the elementary school before anyone realized that Ben had brought the rabbits with us.

"He's got *both* of them back there?" Mom asked, turning all the way around. "I thought we were going to give them to —"

"It's okay," Dad said.

Sally started to sing a one-note, one-word song: "Fluff, Fluff, Fluff, Fluff."

Laura woke up and joined in: "Fluff, Fluff, Fluff, Fluff."

Then Mom and Dad were talking about directions. Mom had an atlas on her lap and was saying something about I-74 to I-57 to I-24 to I-65.

"And I four!" Sally yelled.

I glanced over at Clara. She was facing the window. Before we left home, she had changed into blue corduroy Levi's and a gray hooded sweatshirt.

Is she crying?

I turned and looked out my window. I squinted at the streetlights until they became like Christmas tree lights. We drove past St. Jude's. The video store. The library. The movie theater.

The streetlights grew farther and farther apart as we approached the edge of the city. I kept squinting, blinking, trying to make my eyes swallow the infuriating tears I could feel forming.

We drove past Bargain Bonanza. I realized then that I hated that store with every bone in my body.

We drove past the sign that had first defined, then later cursed, my childhood: THANKS FOR BEING NORMAL!

Yeah, thanks.

Ben was wide awake and waving from the cargo area: "So long, Normal, you big people pooper-scooper. You big knuckle-head! Hey, Laura, 'member when I called you a knucklehead and you thought I said 'bucklehead'?"

Ben whooped with laughter. Laura was laughing, too. Even Dad chuckled a little.

"But Dad," yelled Ben. "That's what she said: buckle-head! Man, that was funny. That was so funny."

"Okay," Dad said. "Settle down back there."

Ben continued laughing, snorting, whispering to himself. "I said 'knucklehead,' but she thought I said 'bucklehead.'" He began quietly humming to himself and giggling softly.

Then, he bolted straight up and yelled at full volume, "Hey, Laura! Fluff's peeing! Awwwww, CRAP!"

Mom's head swiveled around: "Ben!"

"I meant CRUD!"

Jeez, this was going to be a long trip.

But I couldn't help turning to look at Ben. When I did, I saw Clara's face, turning back toward her window. Our eyes met mid-turn. It was only for a second, but I could see that her eyes were turned up at the corners. Smiling eyes!

Thank God for Ben. He could make anyone laugh.

I was staring out my window as we drove away from Normal. I readjusted my focus until I could see my reflection in the glass. I looked old and scary, almost devil-y, like a Bargain Bonanza clown gone bad.

I needed a prayer. A different prayer. So I made one up:

Give us this day our daily bread and forgive us our trespasses as we forgive those who trespass against us and lead us not into temptation but deliver us from evil.

Deliver us from Normal. Get us out of here. Get us out of this godforsaken place. Please. Thank You.

Amen.

BOOK TWO

17.

When I woke up, the sky was mottled pink. We were pulling into a McDonald's drive-through.

Mom was driving. Dad was trying to find exact change for two coffees without waking Sally. Clara was eating a breakfast bar. Laura had the sluggishness of the recently wakened and fed. Traces of chocolate clung to the edges of her mouth. Ben was snoring his familiar white noise growl behind me.

I scrunched the pillow someone (*Mom?*) had given me somewhere (*Mattoon?*) in the middle of the night. I used it as a wedge between my head and the padded plastic of the car door panel.

I fell back asleep. When I woke up again, I looked at my watch. It was just past seven o'clock.

Clara and Laura were chewing gum. Ben was talking to his action figures.

"You dare say that to *me?* Well then, we'll just see about *that!*" Sound of plastic hitting plastic. "I take it back! Sorry, too late." Plastic hitting plastic.

Clara saw that I was awake, and reached in a grocery bag at her feet.

"Chums?" she asked, showing me a chocolate chip granola breakfast bar in a red foil wrapper.

"Oh, yeah. Thanks."

She tossed it to me, overhand. I opened it and chewed quietly.

Dad turned around from the front seat and handed a magazine back to Clara and me.

"Take a look," he said.

The magazine was opened to the second-to-the-last page. An ad was circled several times with a black marker.

"Read it out loud?" Clara said.

I read the tiny text:

BARGE HOUSEBOAT (20′ × 8′2″). FREEDOM AND ADVENTURE SEEKERS ONLY! WANT TO GET AWAY FROM THE DOG-EAT-DOG WORLD? THEN ESCAPE TO THE WATER IN THIS COZY VESSEL. SLEEPS FOUR, WITH SETTEES CONVERTING INTO DOUBLE BERTHS. HEAD HAS SHOWER; PRIVATE ENTRANCE. FULL STANDING HEADROOM IN GALLEY. EQUIPPED WITH COOKSTOVE. OUTBOARD MOTOR. IN-BOARD ENGINE. BEEN AROUND THE BLOCK A TIME/TWO, BUT HAVEN'T WE ALL? IDEAL FOR RECREATION OR RETIREMENT. DON'T WANT TO LEAVE HER IN THE WATER YEAR-ROUND? BRING HER HOME (EASY TOW ON FLATBED TRAILER) AND USE AS GUEST ROOM OR MOTHER-IN-LAW QUARTERS. OWNER ILL. MUST SELL IMMEDIATELY. $49,400 OBO. CURRENTLY DOCKED IN FAIRHOPE, ALA. WILL SHARE TOWING COSTS. CONTACT MSSR. PLATTINBONQUE FOR DETAILS.

And below that was a grainy photograph and a phone number.

"So it's a houseboat?" Clara asked Dad.

"Yeah."

"Cool," said Clara.

"Houseboat?" asked Laura, like this was a riddle. "Is it a *house* or a *boat?*"

"It's both," said Clara.

Laura turned and looked at me with her *Is-this-a-joke-and-you're-all-making-fun-of-me?* face.

"Well, I don't get it," Laura said. "Is it half a boat and half a house? Which part is which?"

Clara folded her torso and pulled her blue plastic tackle box from under the front seat. She unlatched it and retrieved a small spiral sketchbook and a pencil.

"Let me try to draw one," she said, making tentative lines on the paper. "I don't really know what a houseboat looks like. Chums, let me see the picture, will you?"

I did.

"Oh, see?" said Clara. "Look, Laura. This is neat."

I asked Clara if I could borrow a piece of paper from her sketchbook.

"And a pen, too?"

She gave me both. I began to make a list.

Plan for Our New Life

No more work (M/D)	what about $$?
No more school (kids)	law? till 16? 18?
No more neighbors (all)	ok
No more yard work (all)	ok
No more housework (all)	boatwork worse?
No more homework (kids)	library? books — where?
No more classmates (kids)	fine

Across the bottom of the list, I wrote: *Live on houseboat and sail around the world! New Life!*

The forced cheeriness of the last line reminded me of those scrolling messages on the light fixture at church (TEENS SIGN UP NOW FOR WEEKEND OF FUN & SPIRITUALITY AT TEEN-ONLY LOCK-IN!!).

I crossed out the exclamation marks on my plan. Then I crossed out the entire last line. If this didn't work, I didn't want to leave a paper trail of my misplaced optimism.

Clara was still sketching houseboats when Laura said, "I think I forgot my toothbrush!"

And then from behind us: "Oops! Me too."

Clara tossed a breakfast bar back to Ben.

"Can I see a picture of our boat?" he asked.

Clara handed the magazine to him. He struggled to read the ad copy. ("Then *escappy* to the water in this *cuzzy* vessel.")

"Why'd they call it a 'her'?" Ben asked.

"I dunno," I said. "They just do that with boats."

"Oh. What's a 'M S S R'?" he asked, his mouth full of chocolate-covered oats.

"*Monsieur,*" I said. "It means a French man."

"Oh. Okay."

Ben passed the magazine back to me and returned to his private world of action figure drama.

"Howdy there, *mon-seer,*" he began. "How'd you like to c'mon over to my ranch here and see my horses?" (Pause. Then a deeper voice:) "Don't mind if I do, *pardner.*"

Laura sat on her knees and turned around toward Ben. She made a peace sign with her hand and moved it — small, timid jumps — along the top of the seat.

"Hi, *mon-seer,*" she said in a tiny voice to Ben's plastic characters. "I'm just a little blind bunny girl. Wanna come over to my houseboat?"

"Well, sure, li'l blind bunny girl," Ben answered grandly. "*Mon-seer'n* I'd love to come over to your li'l old houseboat gal. We'll just mosey on over."

I paged dully through the entire boating magazine before noticing the sticker on the front cover: NORMAL PUBLIC

LIBRARY FRIENDS OF THE LIBRARY FALL BOOK SALE. The magazine was three years old.

I began drawing crosshatches through my *Plan for Our New Life.* Definitely no paper trail on this.

18.

The front seat sounded like a daylong bingo marathon as Mom and Dad looked for I-65 South to Highway 287, and then 59 to 31 to 181 to I-10 to U.S. 90/98.

We passed exits for odd-sounding cities: Goodlettsville, Pleasant View, Tiny Town. I wondered how we'd fit in with the people there. (*We're just a family of little blind bunnies. Can we live with you here in Tiny Town?*)

My dad's favorite was Frankewing, Tennessee. We stopped there for gas. Dad paid with a traveler's check. He had an envelope full of them.

Is that all the money we have? What happens when we run out?

Every twenty minutes or so, I looked at the ad for the houseboat and then at my parents.

Do they know how freakin' old this magazine is?

But I had neither the courage nor the energy to ask my most worrisome questions. Finally, as northern Alabama passed by outside my window, I said to the front seat in as casual a voice as I could feign:

"Forty-nine thousand four hundred dollars?"

"O B O," said Dad. "That stands for 'Or Best Offer.' This Plattinbonque fella is really sick. So he was willing to come way down."

"How far?" I asked, again casually, as if this were the kind of conversation Dad and I had all the time.

And then I said, "Heck, just give me two THOUSAND shares of AT&T if you can get it for THAT!"

"Well," Dad said, "I told him the best offer we could make was $3,500 and our car and the trailer. And he said okay."

"I still feel terrible taking advantage of him," said Mom. "Imagine selling a houseboat for $3,500 and this old car."

"But if the man's sick, maybe he needs the money for his medicine," Laura chirped.

"Yeah," said Ben. "And if he's really sick, he has to go to the hospital to get better, right? Maybe it will make him happy to know that a nice big family like us gets to ride in his boat while he's at the hospital."

If the guy's sick, I thought, *why does he want a car?* But I said nothing. I sat still as a deer and tried not to cause any more problems for my family.

*　　*　　*

It was almost dark by the time we found our exit: Daphne-Fairhope/Spanish Fort. Dad was driving the last leg of the trip.

"Only ten miles to the boat," he said with equal parts excitement and exhaustion.

"Ten miles!" said Laura. "What *day* is it?"

What day was it? I had orchestra practice on Wednesday. Didn't go to school on Thursday. We left that night.

"Friday," I said, and remembered that Clara's election was today.

She was staring out her window. I wondered if she remembered. I wondered if I should ask. I never even asked how her speech went. I couldn't now.

We passed the Fairhope Senior Center. Fairhope Family Discount Drug. Kidney Dialysis Center of Fairhope.

Fairhope. It sounded like an old-movie town where Dad might grow a handlebar mustache and Mom might start calling us kids "my little darlings."

Or maybe not.

"Okay, Magellan, then *you* find Volanta Avenue on this map," Mom growled at Dad.

It was after six o'clock when we finally arrived at the address Mssr. Plattinbonque had given Dad. It was a trailer across the street from a marina.

"He said he's either in his office or at the marina most days from eight till five," Dad said.

Silence.

"Can we call him?" Mom asked.

Dad disappeared to find a pay phone. The rest of us stumbled out of the car.

"Mom, can I run down and look at the boats?" Ben asked.

"Be careful."

Ben took off at a gallop.

"Can me'n Sally go, too?" Laura asked.

"Have one of the big kids help you cross the street."

Clara and I both went.

"This is just like a giant parking lot — for boats!" Laura said, skipping down the pier.

"Look at this one!" Ben yelled, five or six boats in front of us. "I wonder if our boat looks like this!"

It was a pilothouse power cruiser that cost twice as much as the most expensive house in Normal.

"Oh! Look at this pretty one!" Laura cooed, standing in front of a lovingly restored classic wooden sailboat. It was painted British racing car green and had crisp white sails that snapped in the breeze. It reminded me of a model sailboat I'd seen once in a pricey Christmas catalog of toys for grown-ups.

I breathed in the smells of the dock and tried to identify the various components: *seaweed, paint, money, success, happiness.*

I turned around and saw Mom and Dad in the distance. Dad was making an open-palmed gesture that I knew meant:

I know but that's what he said, and what can we do? Mom was walking away from him, toward us, while he was still talking.

Oh, God. Don't let them be fighting. Please don't fight.

"Mom," Laura cried, running toward her with Sally on her heels. "Ben says our boat is going to be a big creepy pirate ship."

"I said I *hoped* it was a pirate ship!" Ben hollered, bouncing behind her, his eyes filled with hope and a strange delight. "This place is *SO* cool!"

"Isn't it?" Mom agreed enthusiastically. But only her mouth smiled. Her eyes and jaw were set hard, like a soldier statue in a war cemetery.

"Let's go!" yelled Laura.

"Yeah, let's go!" echoed Sally.

The two girls held hands and jumped around in a circle, chanting, "Let's go! Let's go! Let's go! Let's go!"

"Now, just a minute," Mom said in her *Everyone-settle-down* voice. "The man we were supposed to meet has gone home. He can't come back tonight to let us see our boat."

"Awwwwwwwwwwwwww."

"It's okay," Mom continued. "Because he'll be here at eight o'clock in the morning, and we can see our boat then."

"But what about tonight?" Laura asked. "Where're we gonna sleep tonight?"

"Well," said Mom. "It's almost seven o'clock now. So we've

only got about twelve hours. There's no sense wasting money on an expensive motel room. I'm thinking we could have a *snackasbord* dinner and just curl up in the car. That way, we'll be right here when the man comes back in the morning."

"*Snackasbord?*" asked Ben, his face a comic contortion. "What's a *snackasbord?*"

"It's like a smorgasbord," explained Mom, "except it's all snacks."

Ben had slipped his body under Mom's left arm. Laura and Sally hung on to her right.

"Like peanut butter and crackers," Mom continued. "And apple slices. And maybe pretzels or cookies."

The flatness in her voice was lost on my younger siblings. They heard only Mom's words (*"Sure we can have snacks for dinner!"*) and not the secret meaning hidden below (*"We are on the brink of a major crisis!"*) that I alone could hear.

Laura and Sally resumed their chanting with a slight variation: "Snackasbord, snackasbord, snackasbord!"

Ben chimed in: "All aboard, snackasbord! All aboard, snackasbord!"

The cheers turned to tears in short order when, while eating in the car, Ben asked Dad if tomorrow night for dinner we could roast Mrs. Fluff.

"I was *kidding*," Ben insisted to Laura, who had pulled

her T-shirt over her face and refused to look at him. "Some people can't take a joke!"

Mom tried to change the subject.

"Hey, we've got a big decision to make," she said, with an enthusiasm I didn't buy. "Every boat has a name. Let's think about what we should call our boat."

Dad suggested *The Majestic.*

"Simple, but classic," he explained. "Or maybe *Frank's Ark.* Eh? What do you think?"

"How 'bout *The Great Explorers*?" said Ben.

"I think we should call it *The Fluff*," said Laura, glaring at Ben. "Or *The Taob*. That's boat backwards. Or *Snackasbord*."

"To sound like a real ship, I think the name should begin with S.S.," Mom said, smearing an orange cracker with peanut butter and handing it to Sally. "Maybe the S.S. *Seven Suitcases.* That sounds like one of your mystery books, Charles."

"Mmmmmmm," I mumbled. "Kinda."

"Why not just *The Harrisong*?" asked Clara. "It's a pretty name. Or maybe the *Free at Last.* Or *The Dream* — since we're in Alabama."

Alabama! I'd forgotten. I wondered if we were far from Finch's Landing.

After we ate, Mom created sleeping nests out of blankets and pillows for Ben, Laura, and Sally in their respective places in the car.

When everyone was tucked in, we drove across town to a twenty-four-hour discount grocery store called ShopWorld. Dad parked near the back of the lot. He turned the engine off.

Ben and Sally were already asleep. Laura was heading that way. Mom said she was going for a walk. Dad followed her.

I sat in the backseat with Clara — Laura between us — and watched the hypnotizing parade of people gliding in and out of ShopWorld. In empty handed. Out with bags. In with nothing. Out with something.

"Remember that ant farm we sent away to Arizona for?" I said, not turning from the window.

"Yeah," said Clara. "Exactly. Only the opposite."

To my surprise, Clara fell asleep minutes later, her curls smashed against the headrest. The fact that she could sleep was a positive sign, I thought. We were getting away from Normal. We were putting it all behind us. This was good.

Then again, my brother and sisters were sleeping in our car in a parking lot and my parents were God knows where.

Welcome to Peculiar, where the ODDS aren't necessarily with you.

19.

The next morning, after washing our faces in the Shop-World restrooms, we returned to the Volanta Avenue address.

At seven o'clock, ours was the only car in the three-car parking lot. Clara and I took the little kids down to the marina again. We tried to guess which boat was ours.

"It's hard to tell from the picture," Clara said as we walked along the pier.

An hour later an old yellow Cadillac pulled in the parking lot. A leathery-looking man with an enormous stomach maneuvered with some difficulty out of the car. I saw handshakes. Heads nodding. Pointing to us. Then my mother, waving us back.

"We've got to drive to another marina," Mom explained when we piled in.

"Is that him?" I asked Dad as he pulled behind the yellow Cadillac.

"Yep," Dad said, and he handed a business card back to me.

RALPH PLATTINBONKERS
PURVEYOR OF FINE SAILING VESSELS FOR BUSINESS OR PLEASURE
FAIRHOPE   POINT CLEAR

I studied the card and handed it to Clara. She looked at it and then at me. I stuck out my bottom lip and shrugged. Ben grabbed the card from Clara. "Ralph Blubberbutt," he said.

Mom's head turned on its axis: "Dammit, Ben! Stop it."

Oh, my God. Mom never loses her temper this much.

The car was silent for the entire ten-minute ride. I updated my *Things to Worry About* list:

Our financial situation
Mom and Dad fighting
The fact that none of us knows anything about boats
Plattinbonque/Plattinbonkers (Surely this guy is a con artist.)
Me and my straight-A record for ruining things

We drove down a dirt road, past a dump and a dog kennel (GUARD DOGS FOR SALE — WILL TRAIN).

Ralph Plattinbonkers drove agonizingly slow. Maybe it was to avoid kicking up dust, or maybe to protect his low-riding car. Or maybe just because it was his style, like pulling his Cadillac way left before making an easy right turn.

We returned to a paved road. I saw the water again. *Where were we?* I was completely disoriented. We pulled into a gravel parking lot. A wooden sign with the words BOAT YARD painted in faded blue letters hung precariously on a metal fence.

"Sorry about that road," Mr. Plattinbonkers yelled over to us. He was sliding ungracefully out of his car. "I like to take shortcuts whenever possible. Avoid the traffic on the main drag."

Plattinbonkers asked Dad to hold a file folder while he used both arms to drag the metal fence over a pile of gravel.

"Allrightie," he said, taking the file back from Dad. "Let's see where we are. Slip 42. All the way in the back."

Ben bolted from the rest of us. Laura and Sally followed behind him, running.

I stayed back and listened to Dad and Mr. Plattinbonkers discuss things I didn't understand: titles, transfers, licenses. I noticed Mr. Plattinbonkers began almost every sentence with "All you hafta do" or "Why, that's nothing more than" or "Nobody with a right mind would . . ."

Mr. Plattinbonkers stretched the word *right* to two syllables with a long fat "i" in the middle and an easy "d" at the end: *riiiiiiiiiiiiiiiide.*

I wondered if our minds were riiiiiiiiiiiiiiiiide. (*"Those*

Harrisongs. They never were normal, and you know why? Their miiiiiiiinds weren't riiiiiiiiiiiiiiiiide.")

I hadn't been in the South a full day and already I was thinking with an accent.

This boatyard had a different feel entirely from the Volanta Avenue marina. The air was different. The smell of — *what was it? dirty socks?* — clung to everything. And someone was cooking something — *bacon? beans?* — on one of the boats.

I looked in the water and saw two beer cans floating next to a bloated fish. A gull was pecking furiously at an empty bag of Lay's KC Masterpiece Barbecue Potato Chips stuck in the pier.

And the boats! They were nothing like the sleek racing creatures at the first marina. Where were the pristine sails? The glistening hulls? These boats were fat and squatty, like floating trailers.

We passed slips 29, 30, 31, 32. I read the names on the boats: *The Jeff & Linda. The Good Old Boys. The Thursday Nighters. The Gumbo Pot.*

Oh, I knew where we were: the Bargain Bonanza boatyard. Of course.

I looked ahead and saw Ben, Laura, and Sally standing and pointing.

"*That's* not it," Laura was telling Ben.

"It says '42' right there," Ben said.

"Yeah, but that's not it," Laura insisted. "That boat's a stinker!"

A stinker, indeed. It stunk. Of rotten wood. Of cigarette butts floating in pools of water on the deck. Of dead fish. Of despair. Defeat. Death.

The boat sat low in the water and looked like nothing more than a wooden platform with a wall built around the perimeter and a shed attached to the top. The exterior was an unfriendly dark gray wood with faint hints of green. (Was that *mildew?*) A ratty canoe hung on one side, like Dad's ladder used to hang on the side of his truck.

Mr. Plattinbonkers chose not to respond to Ben's and Laura's initial assessment of this fine sailing vessel. He spoke only to Dad.

"Well, here she is!" Plattinbonkers said with the sincerity of a game show host. "No one in their right mind would move into 'er like *this*. All you hafta do is get a pressure washer out here and blast all that muck off. Why, nothing more than fifty bucks to rent a pressure washer for the day."

He handed Dad the file folder and began explaining the permits we'd need. And how Sharon's the woman in the office you need to talk to. Nobody else in that place knew what they were doing. But Sharon, now, *she'd* fix us right up. Yes, she would. All you hafta do is . . .

Our previous night's conversation echoed in my mind like that jeering jack-in-the-box in my brain: *The Majestic. The Dream.* The storybook-sounding S.S. *Seven Suitcases.*

"Oh my gosh," Mom said, wiping sweat from her forehead.

Dad was fumbling with the file. "This is not exactly what we —"

"Y'all said there was no need to view the property before agreeing to the terms of the purchase," Mr. Plattinbonkers said, sloppily tucking his shirt in his pants. "And under Alabama law —"

They had bought this piece of trash without seeing it?

"But from the way you described it on the phone and in the ad —" Dad began.

Mom interrupted. "You told Frank there were all kinds of people who wanted to buy this boat," she said mechanically, through clenched teeth. "And if we didn't agree to the terms of the contract right then, the boat'd be gone."

"It woulda been," said Plattinbonkers. "I coulda sold this boat all day long."

Mr. Plattinbonkers laughed. A little bubble of spit clung to the corner of his mouth.

They bought a boat from this joker over the phone? They'd

agreed to a contract without even having a lawyer look at it? People, THINK!

I heard several gulls — *CAW CAW CAW* — now claiming rights to the empty potato chip bag. Their cry reminded me of the sinister *ERK, ERK, ERK* of all those broken shopping carts back home. All those popular kids laughing at us. Victor Wolfe. Randy Breedlove. And now this boat — not even a *real* boat but a cartoon boat with its pouty mouth and snarling eyebrows — mocking us.

"Look," Dad said, forcing a smile. "You can't expect me to trade our car — which I can tell you right now has a better engine in it than this thing — today. I'll need it to pick up supplies. Lumber. The pressure washer. Everything."

They discussed a plan: $3,500 in traveler's checks today; the car in a week. *Not a week. Three or four days is all you need to clean 'er up. Look at these rotten floorboards! All you hafta do is. Think of the risk. My children! Safety! Well, you got a house somewhere, don't you? Nobody in their riiiiiiiide miiiiiiiind would thinka doing this with five little ones. . . . Two weeks. One week. Ten days. A week from Sunday.*

Dad and Mr. Plattinbonkers continued to negotiate while the rest of us stared at the filthy floating trailer that was our new home.

"This is the S.S. *El Stinko*," Ben said, kicking a wooden post.

I could think of a million names for this boat: *The Bargain Bonanza. The Christmas in August. The Little Match Girl. The Vincent van Gogh as a One-Eared Rabbit. The Boo Radley.*

I looked at Clara and whispered, *"The Boo Radley."*

She bit her lip and nodded.

"Oh my gosh," Mom said again. Now her mouth was smiling, but her eyes were wet with anger.

"Hey, that's it!" Laura said cheerily. "That's what we'll call it: The S.S. *Oh My Gosh.* Because that's what all our friends will say when they see it: Oh my gosh!"

Mr. Plattinbonkers was counting Dad's traveler's checks. Then he was pumping Dad's hand and walking away.

When Plattinbonkers was still within shouting distance, Ben hollered at him: "Hey, Mister!"

Ralph Plattinbonkers turned around. "Yes?"

Ben yelled back: "Are you sick?"

Plattinbonkers put one hand over his chest. I could see he was making that odd smiling frown face.

"Be a good boy," Plattinbonkers hollered back, and continued on his way.

Ben looked at Dad with a *What the —?* expression.

Plattinbonkers continued walking toward his big yellow Cadillac. Ben wasn't quite finished.

"Hey, sir! What's your real name?"

Plattinbonkers turned around again.

"In the magazine," yelled Ben. "It said you were a *mon-seer*."

"Oh, yes!" Plattinbonkers said. He was now walking toward us with a big happy cat smile on his face.

"Plattinbonque," he said, hyper-enunciating the last syllable. "My family's Cajun. Acadian. I use the Anglicized version for business. Plattinbonkers."

Ben turned away from him and faced the water.

"*Mon-seer,* my butt," he said, under his breath.

Clara laughed softly.

She was feeling better, I thought. At least Clara was feeling better.

20.

We left the boatyard and went to ShopWorld for cleaning supplies, milk, eggs, ice, and toothbrushes for Laura and Ben. The bill came to $38.87. Dad peeled off two twenties from the stack of traveler's checks.

From there we went to HomeLand, a sprawling building supply center (OUR HOME IS YOUR HOME!). We filled a cart with lumber, nails, engine degreaser, epoxy, and work gloves for all of us. Dad tossed six traveler's checks on the counter as if he were dealing cards for a game of gin rummy.

How much of this Monopoly money is left? How long can this go on?

We spent the rest of the day hauling trash off the S.S. *O'Migosh,* as we were now calling our houseboat, much to Laura's delight, and mainly to avoid another tsunami. Laura's feelings had been hurt when we considered other names. ("No one ever likes *my* ideas. No one ever listens to *me.*")

We filled more than fifty trash bags with the previous owners' garbage: bottles, dishes, rusty silverware, an umbrella, rotten boards, a broken fishing pole, pink sponge hair curlers, dirty clothes, a doll with no head, a plastic purse.

Much of the stuff wouldn't fit in bags. So we carried these things any way we could — a broken lawn chair rode on my back; a waterlogged mattress teetered on top of the station wagon — and heave-hoed them over the edge of a Dumpster we found on a dirt road across from the boatyard.

On the fourth trip back from the Dumpster, I noticed that I'd misread the sign on the metal fence. It didn't say BOAT YARD. It was BONE YARD.

Naturally.

"Hey, look at this!" Ben said when I returned to the boat. He was wearing a raggedy old cloth fishing hat he'd found belowdeck.

Ben was the first among us to brave the rickety wooden ladder that led from the deck down below. There we found a rank kitchenette, a dining area that became a sleeping area at night (*Oh, so that's what settees were: vinyl benches*), and a bathroom too offensive to describe.

No, the bathroom deserves description if only to say that removing the half-rotted rat from the toilet — those Herculean smells! — was not the worst job during those first days of our New Life. (And no, Ben's suggestion as we were carrying the rat on a board and then hurling the bloated, dripping carcass over the side of the Dumpster — *"Hey, Charles, just pretend like it's pretend!"* — didn't help.)

Mom spent the day in the galley, trying to transform it into a functioning kitchen. Dad showed her how to unlatch the table on hinges so that it could be folded down for meals and returned to the wall at non-meal times.

Clara and Mom fixed scrambled eggs for dinner, which we ate with crackers off paper plates while sitting in a patch of grass next to the Bone Yard parking lot.

"This is sorta like a picnic, isn't it?" Ben said to no one in particular.

No response.

"You know how I know?" he continued, ever undeterred. "'Cause a bug just flew in my mouth. And that *always* happens when you're on a picnic."

"Hey, Mom," Laura said, suddenly enthused. "'Member that time at the school picnic when Ben got in trouble for throwing water balloons?"

Ben threw a cracker at Laura, who scampered away and began filling her hands with gravel.

"Hey," Dad said. "None of that."

"But, Dad!" Laura wailed. "HE started it!"

"I did NOT!"

"*Enough!*" Dad barked in his once-a-year mad voice.

We ate the rest of the meal in silence.

After dinner, Mom returned to the station wagon and re-created the sleeping nests for Ben, Laura, and Sally. Clara pitched the tent next to the car. She and Mom slept in it. Dad said he wanted to sleep on the boat.

He hung utility lights on nails so he could work late, replacing rotten floorboards. I heard the sound of him pounding nails (*Dang Dang Dang Dang*) until after midnight, when I crawled back in the car.

Laura was sprawled out in the backseat lengthwise, so I had to sleep sitting up. I stretched my legs as far under the front seat as they'd go. My feet hit the boating magazine. I pulled it out and held the page with the circled ad up to the open window. By the light of the moon, I reread the description of our new home: *Freedom and Adventure Seekers Only . . . Want to get away from the dog-eat-dog world . . . Cozy vessel . . . Been around the block a time/two, but haven't we all? . . . Ideal for recreation or retirement . . . Don't want to leave her in the water year-round? Bring her home (easy tow on flatbed trailer) and use as guest room or mother-in-law quarters.*

Oh. So basically this was a floating trailer that you could park in your backyard and stick an unwanted relative in.

How could my parents have been so guileless? So trusting. So believing.

No, say what you're really thinking:

So *stupid*.

I fell asleep and dreamed that I was fishing. I caught something. When I reeled it in, I saw it wasn't a fish, but a wooden sign with words crudely painted on it: FREE HOUSEBOAT. ANYBODY WANT THIS WORTHLESS OLD SCRAP PILE? CALL RALPH PLATTINBONKERS AT THE BONE YARD FOR DETAILS.

In my dream, Ben was with me. When he read the sign, he said, "Why, that no-good cheating son-of-a —"

"Watch your mouth, young man," Dad said. I hadn't realized he was there.

"Wait," said Clara, turning the sign over. "There's something written on the back."

There was. The flip side of the sign said: ANYBODY WHO'D WANT THIS PIECE OF TRASH IS CRAZY!

I recognized the handwriting. Whose was it?

Oh, of course. Sister Theresa Paul.

I woke up with a jolt. It was dark. I couldn't see the numbers on my watch, but I could hear my heart pounding furiously — *DangDangDangDangDangDang.*

We were crazy, I thought. That's why we're white trash. Why we'd never be normal or lucky or rich. It was all becoming painfully clear to me. We were the kind of people whose lives never worked out. We were the families you read about in the newspapers who lose everything in a fire. Then they build back, and a one-hundred-year flood wipes them out. We were the freaks of nature who were destined to wake up with fast-moving diseases. Unheard-of diseases. Strange growths inside our bodies.

I closed my eyes and imagined the scene in the hospital. "A tumor as big as *the New York City phone book?*" I'd say, lying in a hospital bed in my Bargain Bonanza underwear and a matching neckerchief. "But I thought tumors were always round and the size of grapes or walnuts or oranges."

Normally, that's true, the kind doctor would say, a sporty stethoscope draped around his neck. And the nurse would look at me with big, gentle eyes. (*Why couldn't my dad be a doctor? Why couldn't my mom be a nurse?*)

But this a not a normal tumor.

Of course it wasn't normal. We were Harrisongs. Nothing we did was normal.

And abnormal tumors are very expensive to treat, the doctor explained. *Given the fact that your family doesn't own a house or a car.*

Or an air conditioner, the nurse added, her chin perched on a clipboard. And she smiled with that happy-sad-faced expression that I was learning people used to show pity.

The doctor sighed, shaking his head slowly.

Or an air conditioner, he finally said. And he squeezed my hand gently.

And then I saw Mrs. Flanagan in the hospital bed next to me.

"If it were *my* houseboat," she hissed, "I'd burn it using the dried bones of that snot-nosed Little Match Girl for kindling."

I woke up, gasping for air. My heart was hammering harder and louder (*DANG DANG DANG DANG DANG*), right at the surface of my chest. I tried to calm myself by reviewing what I knew was true.

I was in Alabama. I was sitting in our car. The car was parked near a boat that was our new home. Only the boat was more like a trailer. The ocean was more like a sewer. And a rat had drowned in our toilet.

Now I understood. This was one of my haunted house mysteries gone wrong. It was a mockery of everything I loved. Instead of gentlemanly dark-paneled libraries, hidden staircases, and talking owls, my options have devolved to their filthy opposites:

To peek under the rotten floorboard,
  turn to page 161.
To climb the wooden ladder — watch out for
  missing rungs! — down to the feces-stained
  bilge, turn to page 162.

To follow the angry gull with the raggedy potato
chip bag in its mouth, turn to page 163.
To find a bag filled with gold — oops, wrong
story — to FILL a plastic garbage bag with
some slob's old mustard and ketchup bottles
and rusty cans of shaving cream (Old Spice,
my butt!), turn the page.

How I wished I could turn the page. On this whole ugly thing.

My stomach made a weird, ghostlike noise. The tumor inside me was shifting, expanding. The wave was swelling. Or was I just hungry?

I must've fallen back to sleep again because when I woke up, I saw Mom standing in the grass, pouring juice into paper cups. She was telling Clara to take Laura and Sally down to the public restrooms on the beach.

"Today we'll rent the pressure washer and clean this baby up," Dad said, sitting in the grass next to Mom and lacing up his work boots.

But today was Sunday, and the U-Rent-It Center was closed. So we spent another day cleaning the S.S. *O'Migosh*. We cleaned ourselves, too (well, sponge baths), in the restrooms at ShopWorld while Dad replumbed the *O'Migosh*.

I waited for Mom to tell us to get ready for church. But she never did. So now we weren't going to church anymore? Had Mom completely given up? This was not good.

Not that I missed church, really. But without it, what was the sense of being meek or poor in spirit? Or poor in traveler's checks, for that matter? Without church, the first would be first and the last would be last, just like in normal life. Just like in Normal.

I remembered the garish light fixture at St. Jude's and those relentless scrolling messages. WITHOUT CHURCH, YOU DON'T HAVE A PRAYER. COMPLIMENTARY MARY KAY MAKEOVERS FOR THE LADIES OF ST. JUDE'S. SEE DOLORES HIGGINS AFTER MASS.

It was all nonsense, I knew. But it was the nonsense I knew. Going to Mass every week was the lottery ticket my mother bought; the small investment that could pay off big.

I guess I always knew we didn't have a chance. But now Mom knew it, too. I'd ruined it for her. And that made me sadder than anything.

21.

Dinner started out better on Sunday night. It was still a picnic on the grass next to the Bone Yard parking lot. But Mom fixed a crowd pleaser: nachos topped with heated chili from a can, cheese, sour cream, and lettuce.

"This is what I *really* wanted to have at my birthday party," Laura said, pulling a chip with a long cheese tail from the congealed mound of tortilla chips. "Mom, can I have this next year for my birthday? *Please?*"

"Me too!" Ben added, smacking his lips. "Just nachos and cake. That'd be so great. You wouldn't even have to have ice cream."

"You *have* to have ice cream," Laura said indignantly. "At least for my birthday you have to."

"You don't *have* to," Ben said. "You don't *have* to do anything but pay taxes and die. Right, Dad?"

Dad answered with a shrug and a noncommittal grunt.

Clara pulled a cluster of cheese-melded chips from the plate.

"I never gave my report on last Sunday's spirituality service," she said.

Dad swallowed quickly and said, "Sweetie, you don't have to."

"But I *want* to," Clara said. "Lark — you know, the Vision Leader? — gave us a really cool image to work on."

"Tell us," Mom said.

"Okay," began Clara. "You start by closing your eyes and turning off the noise in your head. Turn off everything in your mind. If it helps, you can picture yourself turning switches off to school, work, whatever."

We all closed our eyes. I could hear someone's teeth grinding chips. *Ben.* And the sound of a plastic knife cracking. *Mom.*

"So you're getting clear, right?" Clara continued, chewing. "This is really good, Mom."

"Thanks, honey."

"Okay," Clara said. "So now I want you to go to the quiet place in your heart. To get there, you just have to think of someone you love. It can be anybody. A friend. A relative. It can be —"

"I'm picking Jesus and Karenna," Ben announced.

"*Karenna?* Who's Karenna?" Mom asked.

"She's that pretty lifeguard at the pool," Ben said. "She said I do the best belly flops in Normal."

"*Pretty?*" Dad said.

(*Oh, great. Now this?*)

"Ben was Karenna's favorite in the Guppy class," Clara explained to the rest of us. And then in a stage-whisper to Ben: "She told me you were a demon with a kickboard."

I opened one eye. Everybody else's were still closed. Ben's mouth was curled into a sly smile. He looked like a happy golden retriever. Dad was smirking, too. Mom was shaking her head with a *Ben-had-high-school-girls-flirting-with-him?* look on her face.

Clara continued: "So pick Jesus and Karenna —"

"Can it be a rabbit?"

Laura, of course.

"It can't be a *rabbit!*" Ben said. "It has to be a person."

Heavy breathing bordering on tears.

"Ben," said Mom.

"I was just telling Laura the rules! I thought we all had to play by the same rules!"

"Of course it can be a rabbit," said Clara. "No more telling who or what anybody's thinking about. It can be anyone or anything. Just pick whatever works for you. Someone or something you love completely. And remember how you feel when you're together. And now picture him or her — or it or them or whatever — in your mind and hold that image. Look at it and listen to it till your heart starts to feel warm, like it's kind of glowing. Because this is how you listen to your heart."

"I thought this was heartburn."

"Frank."

"Sorry."

"Mom and Dad, c'mon," Clara said. "Try. This is important. You're listening to your heart now. You're remembering a place that feels completely good and pure."

Silence. The sound of everyone's hearts glowing except mine. I was lousy at this stuff. I couldn't think of anything to pick. My mind was too cluttered, like our old junk drawer in the pantry. I thought about asking for more time, but didn't.

"And now this is where you start building on the image," Clara said. "Okay, so I want you to imagine your life as a house. It can be any kind of house you want. Old. New. Brick. A houseboat. Whatever. It can be a tree house, if you want. Everybody got that?"

"Yeah."

"Yes."

"Yep."

"Yeah."

"Mmmm mmmmm."

"Now," Clara said, "the thing about this house is that it has only four rooms: a mental room, an emotional room, a physical room, and a spiritual room. Okay? So now I want you to visualize yourself going in each room. Find a chair or a sofa. And sit down and just look around. And —"

Clara took another loud *chomp* of nachos.

"Well, here's the basic idea," she said, her mouth full. "Lark says most of us have these houses. I mean, we *are* these houses. But we spend all of our time in just one or two rooms. We live in half our house. We don't even decorate the other rooms. So you have to remember to go in every room of your house — mental, emotional, physical, and spiritual — every day, even if it's just to fling the door open and look around and see what's in there."

"What'd you see in your rooms?" I asked.

"Cool stuff," Clara said. "Like old paintings and tapestries and columns and stuff."

"You know what I'm seeing?" said Mom, chewing, her eyes still closed. "I see one of you kids in each of my rooms. Charles, you're in my mental or intellectual room. Ben's all over the physical room. I'm not sure who's in the emotional one, Sally or Laura. Maybe both of you. And in —"

"But I don't *want* to be in the emotional room!" Laura said. "I want to be in the physical room. Why does Ben always get the good *everything?*"

And then Laura got up and ran toward the boat, crying, but *not emotional.*

"Why's Laura cry so dang much?" Ben asked, using the corner of a tortilla chip to transport a large black ant up to his eye level.

"It's just a phase she's going through," said Dad. "She'll get over it."

But Ben's mind was elsewhere.

"Where did Karenna go to school?" he asked dreamily, staring at the ant. Then, out of nowhere: "Hey! Where did *Jesus* go to school?"

"Not in Normal, that's for damn sure," I muttered without thinking.

"*Charles!*" Mom said. "Not in front of —"

"Sorry, I didn't mean that to come —"

"It's okay," Dad said. "Let's clean up these dishes."

We did. In awkward silence.

"I'm sorry," I whispered to Mom, folding my paper plate in the garbage bag she was holding.

"I know," she said. "I just don't like that kind of language from you. Not in front of the little ones."

Ben crushed his plate in the bag, then crossed his arms like his mad scientist alter ego.

"Mom," Ben said, rolling his eyes. "I'm not a baby. I know what *damn* means."

"You do?" asked Dad. He was shaking crumbs off the picnic blanket. "Tell us."

"*Frank!*" Mom said. "Turn the page."

"It's okay," Dad said, attempting a chuckle. "*Damn's* in

the Bible, isn't it? It's in the dictionary. Okay, Ben. So what's *damn* mean? Tell us."

"*Stop it,* Frank," Mom said coldly.

Dad put his hand on Mom's back. "It's okay," he said. "No one's going to hear us. We can talk about this stuff."

Mom sighed loudly. "Okay, Ben," she said. "Tell us what you think it means."

"It means," Ben began earnestly, "'ugly bitch.' Because, Dad, that's what you said that night. Remember? When we went to pick up the chicken and you told me what those kids wrote on Clara's sign? You kept saying it: Damn it to hell. Damn it to hell. Damn it to —"

"I'm gonna go check on Laura," Clara said quickly, stuffing a handful of paper cups in the garbage bag. And then she ran toward the boat.

I watched Mom's face crack as she looked at Dad.

"I'm . . . I'm so sorry," I stammered.

"It's not your fault," Mom said. She was using both hands to strangle the top of the garbage bag.

"She's going to be okay," Dad said softly.

Who? Clara? Mom?

No, they weren't. Neither one of them was going to be okay. And even though Mom didn't say it, I could hear the words she was thinking: *I told you this'd never work. I told you, dammit.*

22.

Like me, Ben had been fishing only once before, with our cousins in Wisconsin. We'd spent four miserable days in the Dells, watching our cousins reel in fish after fish while our lines sat untouched.

But here it was different. Ben convinced Dad to buy him a fishing pole at HomeLand on Monday morning. By Monday afternoon, Ben had caught five fish.

"It's so easy!" Ben said, casting his line from the pier. "Seems like these fish just *wanna* be caught!"

He was still wearing the scruffy hat he'd found on the *O'Migosh*. Only now, it was decorated like a pincushion with the oddball lures he found in a moldy box in the narrow closet next to the no-longer-horrifying-but-still-awful bathroom.

"I thought you were a *cowboy*," Laura said. She was sitting on the pier, washing a skillet in a plastic tub of soapy water.

"Not a cowboy, mate," said Ben, who now spoke with a craggy accent that was impossible to place. "I'm a pirate, I am! *Arrrrrrrrrrrrrrrr.*"

"The only scary thing about you," said Laura, "is the smell of that hat. You could gag a maggot with that hat."

We'd gone from fighting about holes in underwear to stinky hats. In some ways, nothing had changed. In other ways, everything had, including the S.S. *O'Migosh*.

While no one dared credit Ralph Plattinbonkers with the idea, the high-pressure sprayer did wonders for the boat. It washed away the stench, blistered paint, years of filth — and plenty of wood, too. But what was left was at least clean and somewhat sturdy and *ours*.

"We're getting down to the *guts!*" Ben cheered as we watched Dad blast the boat with the sprayer.

"Not the guts," said Clara. "The soul."

When Dad took a break, I heard Clara tell him: "I'm starting to like the looks of this."

"Really?" Dad said.

"Yeah," Clara said, staring at the boat. "Much better than those silly boats at the first dock. Ours is more . . . I don't know what the word is for it. But it looks wiser, doesn't it? Like it has a history. A story to tell."

Dad kissed Clara on the head and said, "Thanks. I like it, too."

I realized suddenly that this was the only home my father had ever bought.

But I knew what Clara meant about the boat. When I

first saw the *O'Migosh,* it had reminded me of a juvenile delinquent. A surly, cigarette-smoking clique leader of bad boats.

Now the raw, weather-beaten wood was beginning to take on a primitive look. Our boat began to remind me of an old woman I saw once at the Greater Normal Mall and Skating Rink. She was Chinese and must've been a hundred years old. But she looked pretty, in a strange way, like she had a secret she'd never tell.

That night, Clara and Mom unpacked the trailer and filled it with blankets and pillows. They called it their *trailerminium* and slept in it with Sally.

Ben and Laura slept in the tent next to the car. Dad worked until 2 A.M. on the boat before stretching out in the backseat of the car. I was in the front seat, editing my list of *Things to Worry About.* I decided that everything basically fell into two categories: 1) What was going to happen to my family, especially Clara? 2) What was going to happen to *me?*

But these were nighttime worries. The daylight hours were filled with chores. Everyone had one or more duties: fishing, sanding, scraping, painting, cleaning, sewing, cooking, or general repairs. Sally's full-time job became feeding Mr. and Mrs. Fluff and singing the one-syllable, one-note song she made up about them, which she called simply: "Fluff."

*   *   *

The days wore on like this. Tuesday. Wednesday. Thursday. Friday. As I watched my family work, I thought how strange it was that something so different from your normal life can become normal so quickly. Wearing the same T-shirt five days in a row. Wearing the same cutoffs every day.

I also saw how my family, like our boat, was getting rawer and more primitive looking as the days passed. Without her lipstick, I could finally see what my mother's mouth really looked like: a long, straight line. Dad, now with a stubbly face, looked stronger, like someone Ralph Plattinbonkers wouldn't want to meet in a dark alley.

With his brown curls turning into dreadlocks, Ben was beginning to look like a modern-day aborigine. Laura and Sally were growing both cuter and mangier; almost feral looking. And Clara's face, with her hair pulled back tightly from it, was getting more angular, almost Egyptian.

They looked different. And yet, they all looked more like themselves.

The only time I saw my own face was in the restroom at ShopWorld. I couldn't describe how I looked. But I know shoppers there didn't look at me and laugh. No one laughed at me or my family. Nobody knew the Normal us here. I liked that.

23.

On Saturday night, we ate our first dinner onboard the *O'Migosh:* baked fish prepared by Mom in the kitchenette we now called the galley and served by the master fisherman himself, Ben, who now had three fishing lines in the water at all times.

"Looky here, mates," Ben said in a pirate accent that was improving somewhat. "If I could just pierce my ear, see, it would help my eyesight. That's why we pirates pierce our ears. Mom, you brought your sewing box — right, matey? You've got a needle in there, I betcha."

He abandoned the accent to explain.

"You remember this, don't you, Mom?" Ben asked. "It was in one of those Great Explorers books. Pirates always pierced one ear 'cause they said it made their opposite eye stronger."

And I'd always thought Ben had slept through those Great Explorer stories.

"Your eyes are fine," Dad said between bites. "Besides, we're not taking any risks with infections. When we shove off, it could be a long time before we're near a doctor or a hospital."

It was the first time anyone had spoken of actually leaving the Bone Yard that had been our home for a week now.

"How soon before we're ready to go?" Mom asked.

Why didn't she look at him anymore when they talked? Not good not good not good.

"Soon," Dad said. "I have just a few more loose ends to tie up."

* * *

Over the next week, Dad made dozens of trips to Home-Land with Laura and Sally tagging along as his helpers. Mom sewed fabric covers for the settee cushions where Clara, Ben, Laura, and I were to sleep. Dad, Mom, and Sally would sleep in the tent they'd pitch nightly on deck.

Clara and I spent every day working belowdeck. I scraped and sanded the worst areas. She painted the whole interior.

"White for now," Clara said. "We can get more creative later."

On Sunday, while Dad worked on the engine, Mom took the rest of us to a rocky beach within walking distance so we could swim. Or rather, so the others could swim. Mom and I stood and watched from the debris-littered beach.

Clara was teaching Sally to float on her back by holding

her like a cafeteria tray and moving her gently through the water. Laura was following Ben's lead of running straight into the water as the tide rolled out, then, turning and running away from it as it crawled back toward shore.

"Mom, look!" Laura shrieked. "The water's chasing me!"

"That wave just bit my butt!" Ben yelled.

"Bottom," Mom said reflexively, in a weary voice too soft for Ben to hear.

I watched my brother and sisters play happily in the water, as if I were watching someone else's home movies.

"Don't you want to cool off in the water, Charles?" Mom asked.

"No. I hate swimming."

Silence.

"Well, just as long as you know *how* to swim," she finally said.

"Of course I know how to swim. Only dummies drown."

Oh, God. Now I was quoting Scoutmaster Breedlove? What next?

On the walk back to the boat, we passed a wooden historical marker: FAIRHOPE WAS FOUNDED IN 1894 BY IDEALISTS FROM IOWA WHO CAME TO THIS SHORE SEEKING UTOPIA. My mind sketched a one-panel cartoon. One Iowan to another: "I told you this'd never work."

Ben found a map under a picnic bench.

"Look! A real live *pirate* map," he said, gazing with wonder at the stained place mat from a local pancake restaurant. The edges of the map had a fake-burnt look. Yellow arrows indicated where chests of gold were buried. Unfriendly islands were marked with grimacing grass-skirted natives.

When we returned to the boat, Ben asked Dad to hang the map up "so we'll know where we're going."

To my surprise, Dad thumbtacked it to the corkboard on the cupboard where we kept Tang, instant coffee, and lemonade mix.

"Show me where are we now," Ben asked.

"Right here," Dad said, sticking one of Mom's sewing pins in the map next to a smiling pink shrimp waving from a beach chair on the Alabama Gulf coast.

"And we're going here," Dad said, gesturing vaguely to a big landmass on the other side of the Atlantic Ocean.

"Where?" asked Ben.

"Wherever we end up," said Dad. "We're going to make our way through the Gulf of Mexico, and then across the Atlantic Ocean until we reach the opposite side."

"And we'll battle pirates by day and make 'em walk the plank at night!" shouted Ben. "We'll watch 'em get ate alive by sharks!"

He laughed the craggy old pirate laugh he'd been working on.

"No, that's *not* what we're going to see," snapped Mom. "And if you *did* see someone get *eaten* alive by sharks, it would be awfully rude to stand by and watch — *laughing,* no less — without trying to help."

"I'm just pullin' your leg, you silly landlubber," Ben said.

"Well, I don't think I'm going," said Laura.

All eyes turned toward her.

"It's just that —"

The volcano was rumbling. The grass-skirted icon was dancing.

"What if we get lost?" Laura whimpered, her kitten-in-a-basket eyes wet with tears. "What if we run out of food? We could *starve* to death!"

Dad squatted and put his arm around her.

"There are risks, honey," he said. "You're right about that. But there were risks back home, too. Our house could've been hit by a tornado. Or I could've gotten sick and not been able to make money to buy groceries —"

Mom interrupted.

"And God knows *I* wasn't pulling *my* weight to support this family," she said. "*I* could never have supported you in the high style your father did."

Mom? What is it? If you don't want to go, either . . .

"I'm just trying to make the point," Dad said, looking first at Mom and then at Laura, "that there were risks back home. And there are risks here."

"But we had *friends* at home," said Laura. The poor thing was trembling.

Dad asked Mom to take a walk with him on the pier. When they returned, it was Mom's turn to make an announcement.

"Laura's right," Mom began. "Crossing the ocean in a boat as old and broken down as —"

"But we fixed it up!" Ben interrupted. "The *O'Migosh* is a first-class ship now!"

"Don't interrupt your mother," Dad said.

Mom continued. "Dad and I have decided that we should take a vote."

"A *vote?!*" Ben shrieked.

"A vote," Mom said, glaring at Ben, "to determine whether we do this or not. We're not going unless it's unanimous."

"That means everyone must agree to go," said Dad. "Or no one goes."

"But . . . but that's not how we did it when we left Normal!" Ben stammered. "The parents decided, and then the kids just did it. We have to do what you say. That's the way it works."

"This is the new way," said Dad.

Ben exhaled as loud as he could. I could see that now *he* was very close to crying.

This family.

"Okay, then," Ben said, pulling Sally's arm up with his own. "Everybody just raise your hand who wants to go."

"No," Dad said as he began tearing a HomeLand receipt into tiny squares. "This will be a secret ballot. No one will know how anyone else voted."

Ben rolled his eyes, and his head followed in a giant loop.

"We spend *aaawwwlllllll* this time fixing up the *O'Migosh* and now we're not even going to *go?* Just because Laura's a scaredy-cat? If Laura doesn't want to go, she can just stay here by herself and go to school!"

"I didn't say I didn't want to GO," Laura protested. "I just said . . . maybe we should go *later.*"

"Okay, that's good," said Dad. "Let's make those our three choices."

Dad wrote three options on the back of seven pieces of the torn-up HomeLand receipt: *Go Now. Go Later. Don't Go.*

"Now," Dad directed, passing around a handful of pencils and pens. "Everybody give this some thought and put your ballot in here." He set a paper cup in the middle of the table.

Ben voted first and loudest. "If we don't get to go just be-cause Laura —"

"If you've voted, go up on deck," Mom said.

"I just meant —"

"NOW!"

Ben crumpled his ballot in the cup and shuffled up the wooden ladder. I deposit my folded ballot in the cup, as did Mom and Sally (*"Which one do I want, Mommy?"*). The three of us climbed up the ladder, followed by Dad.

"Take your time," Dad told Clara and Laura, who remained below.

I stood on the deck and listened to the conversation in the galley.

"If you don't want to go now, that's okay."

"No. I want to go! I just . . . I just don't want anything bad to happen."

"I know. It's all sorta weird. But we'll be together. You'll be okay."

"You're not leaving?"

"No."

The rest was too faint to make out. I could catch just flickers of the conversation:

"But what if we *mumble mumble mumble*. . . . Well, I guess *mumble mumble mumble*. They won't let me take Mrs. Fluff *mumble mumble*. . . . I'll talk to Mom and Dad *mumble mumble*. . . . What if Mom *mumble mumble*. . . . But, Laura, you know *mumble mumble*. . . ."

A few minutes later, Clara and Laura climbed up the

ladder, singing Sally's "Fluff" song. Clara handed the paper cup to Dad.

"I'll count the votes and announce the results at dinner tonight," he said. "In the meantime, let's everybody get back to work."

So we did.

Ben caught more fish (*"I'm telling you, it's this lucky hat!"*). Mom and Laura fixed whole fish baked in Rice-a-Roni for dinner.

After we ate, Dad announced the results of the vote: Don't Go: 0. Go Later: 0. Go Now: 7.

"I knew you'd vote the right way," Ben said, punching Laura in the arm.

"What's left to do?" Mom asked, using her fingers to rake Sally's hair.

When was the last time Mom looked at Dad?

"We're just about ready," Dad said. "We should probably make one more trip to ShopWorld and HomeLand. And after that, it's just a matter of making sure we've got everything we want out of the car and trailer."

"Can we leave tonight?" Mom asked.

Dad hesitated.

"We could," he said slowly. "It'd probably make more sense to wait till morning just in case —"

"I'd rather leave tonight," Mom said flatly, getting up to clear the dishes.

Wait, I thought. *Dad's right. Let's not rush this. Doesn't safety come first? Be careful. Somebody could get hurt. Mom, that's your line.*

"Let's just go," Mom said. (*"Drive, Frank. Can you please just drive?"*)

"Yeah! It'll be like when we left Normal," Ben said. "Everything at night is always ten times more fun!"

And so that was the plan. Dad would take Laura with him to run final errands. Clara, Ben, and I would move all the trailer stuff onto the freshly painted and water-sealed boat. Mom and Sally would clean up from dinner.

"We'll leave the car keys under the floormats," Dad said. "Mr. Plattinwhateverthehellhisnameis will find them eventually."

"Wait!" Laura said as everyone started to get up from the table. "Save your fish bones so we can yell 'Bone Voyage' when we leave."

"Not *bone* voyage," Mom said, and immediately tried to dull the edge in her voice. "It's *bon voyage*. It means 'have a good trip.'"

"I like *bone* better," Laura said meekly. "Because it makes me think of the wishbone. Remember? At Thanksgiving?

How if you got the wishbone, you'd get to make a wish?"

"I like *bone* voyage, too," Clara said. "Let's all make wishes."

"Yeah! Close your eyes, but don't tell what you wish for!" Laura instructed.

So we sat there for a moment, frozen in time. I looked at Dad and could see the shopping list he was making in his head. I looked at Mom, standing next to me, and saw how bone (not *bon*) tired she was.

Clara never looked more peaceful than at these moments, when her eyes were closed and she was someplace else. Laura never looked *less* peaceful than at these same moments, when she was trying (so hard!) to pick the best wish.

Ben, as always, was the portrait of a rock star as a young boy. Or maybe a young Greek god, effortlessly cool in his Chosen Son way. And silly Sally: oblivious to it and us all, forever humming her homage to Fluff song.

I tried to make a wish, but I couldn't help thinking of Thanksgiving back in Normal. Abnormal though we were, we always had turkey and mashed potatoes and gravy and corn bread dressing. I wondered if we'd ever have another Thanksgiving like that. In a way, I wished we would. But I didn't want to waste my wish on something as trivial as an annual turkey dinner. I knew we needed something bigger than that. I needed to wish for something all-encompassing that would include safety, whatever was up with Mom and Dad, as well as my usual repertoire of worries.

Or should I confine my wish to the immediate concerns relating to the boat? There were so many things that could go wrong. How does a heavy wooden boat even float on water, anyway? Maybe I should wish for the laws of buoyancy to be on our side. No. Keep thinking.

"All right, then," Mom said. "Let's get to work. We've got a busy night ahead of us."

And she grabbed my paper plate and smashed it (*Mom!*) on top of her own.

The moment was gone. I couldn't think of the right thing to wish for. So I didn't wish for anything.

24.

It was almost two o'clock in the morning when Dad and I untied the scratchy ropes and released the *O'Migosh* from the dock.

Ben and Laura were asleep down below. Mom was with Sally in the tent we were now setting up nightly on the deck. (Ben and I could put the tent up in seven minutes flat and take it down in the morning in less than three minutes.) Mr. and Mrs. Fluff were nibbling nervously in their cage next to the tent.

Clara was watching Dad and me.

"I'm too excited to sleep," she said as we pushed off.

Dad smiled. His teeth looked yellow in the moonlight. His unshaven face was growing furry in patches. In the two and a half weeks since we'd left Normal, my father had become a different man. Or maybe this was the man he always really was. I wasn't sure I knew him anymore.

Not long before we'd left the dock, Dad had crawled into the tent. I heard him ask Mom: "Don't you think we should wait till morning so Ben and Laura can see us shove off?"

"Let's just *go*," Mom said.

But, Mom, you like us to do everything together. Stand aside and let the little kids see. That's what you used to always say.

So we motored out of the marina. I couldn't believe Ben, Laura, and Sally were able to sleep through the noise. I couldn't understand why Mom wasn't coming out of the tent to see this.

I thought of Midnight Mass.

"Remember last Christmas Eve when we went to Midnight Mass?" I asked Clara.

"Yeah," she said. "What made you think of that?"

"I don't know," I said. "Just that Dad took you and me to Midnight Mass. Then Mom took the little kids to Mass in the morning."

"You're right," said Clara. "It was you and me and Dad that night."

"Yeah," I said. "Remember walking home from church? Just you and me. You wanted to walk because you said the walk would be better than Mass. And looking at the lights in people's houses. Seeing who opened their presents on Christmas Eve and who waited till the morning."

"Uh-huh," Clara said. "Dad let us walk."

"Because he said all the crazies would be at their mothers' house on Christmas Eve."

"And you said, 'I guess that makes us crazy.'"

"And then we came home," I said. "And Mom was mad at Dad for letting us walk home alone."

"She wasn't *really* mad," Clara corrected. "She was just worried."

"I know," I said. "Remember how she let us help bring all the Santa presents downstairs and put them under the tree? Even the stuff for us? And then you and me and Mom and Dad ate the cookies and peanut brittle we left out for Santa."

"Mom made cocoa."

"Yeah," I said. "The real kind with salt."

"Why are you thinking about this, Chums?"

"I dunno. It was just a weird night. Like tonight."

We motored past the Volanta Avenue marina and saw the mansion-like yachts.

"I can't believe we thought we were getting one of those," I said.

"I'm so glad we didn't," Clara said.

"You're serious?"

"Of course," she said. "This is the perfect house."

Just before three o'clock, Clara went down below to sleep. Dad said he was going to stay awake all night and sleep in the morning. I tried to stay awake with him. But a little after four o'clock, I crawled down the ladder and curled up on the cushioned bench across from Ben.

I woke up hours later. Dad was sleeping in a tangled knot on Ben's cushion. I could hear activity up on the deck.

I quietly climbed up the ladder, careful not to wake Dad. Everyone else was awake. Sally and Laura were eating cold cereal from paper cups and laughing. Ben had already caught two big silver fish. Mom and Clara were taking down the tent.

We were floating somewhere, I assumed, in the Gulf of Mexico. It was hard to tell exactly where we were. The fog was as thick as a cloud. It felt strange, almost otherworldly, not to see land in any direction.

Mom gave me two paper cups: one filled with Tang, the other with cold cereal. I ate my breakfast and watched Ben entertain the girls with his pirate imitations.

"And then I told that landlubber, 'Y'ill walk the plank or y'ill DIE!'"

Laura and Sally screamed with delight.

Ben had given up trying to convince Dad to let him pierce his ear with one of Mom's sewing needles. He was now wearing a black eye patch instead. Or, more accurately, he was wearing a raggedy piece of fabric he'd cut from a black sweatshirt I'd thrown in the ragbag. He had it tied around his head with a shoestring.

The plan, Ben said, was that on Mondays, Wednesdays,

and Fridays, he'd wear the patch over his right eye to strengthen his left eye. On Tuesdays, Thursdays, and Saturdays, he'd wear the patch over his left eye to strengthen his right. On Sundays he'd go patch-less to gauge the progress.

He explained all this as he re-baited a fishing line with rice from last night's dinner. He was having difficulty, half-blinded by his patch.

"If that's the plan," Mom said, folding the tent like a bedspread, "you've got your patch on the wrong eye. Today's Tuesday. The patch should be on your left eye."

"It's not Tuesday, you crazy swabbie," said Ben. "Yesterday was Sunday. Today's Monday."

He was struggling with the hook.

"And I'll tell you how I know," Ben continued. "Because when we went swimming yesterday, I found a newspaper in the trash can at the beach. And the comics were in color. And the only day they're in color is Sunday."

"I can tell you guys *exactly* what day it is," Laura said. "Know why? Because I've chewed one inch of gum a day since we left home. And since I wasn't sure how long my gum would last, I've been saving it."

And with that, Laura scooted down the ladder and returned seconds later with a shoebox. She opened it. Inside was a pile of hard, dull-colored wads of gum.

"So all I have to do," Laura explained, "is count the

pieces of my ABC gum in here, and that's the number of days we've been gone."

"ABC gum?" asked Mom.

"Already Been Chewed gum," said Laura, as if speaking to a child half her age. "Let's see. What day did we leave?"

"You think *I'm* gross with my hat?" Ben asked, looking with one eye at the collection of gray gum. "Saving gum is ten times grosser. Twenty times. Even for a landlubber, that's disgusting."

"Fine," said Laura. "See if I share my gum with you ever again."

"You never do anyway," Ben said.

"What day is it?" Mom asked Clara.

"I haven't the foggiest idea," said Clara. "I kind of like not knowing. Don't you?"

"Hey, you rabbits. It's raining down here. On the floor."

It was Sally. She was standing on the middle rung of the ladder.

"What?" said Mom.

"I saw it, too, when I went down to get my gum," Laura offered casually, not looking up from her shoebox. "The floor down there's all wet."

Mom turned to me and stuck her index finger in my chest. "Go wake up your father."

I flew down the ladder in two steps.

"Water? Where?" said Dad.

From the deck we heard Laura screaming, "Are we sinking? We're sinking! We're sinking!"

"No panicking!" hollered Dad. "We all know how to swim. And we have a canoe if we need it."

Ben's voice from the deck: "We'll get ate alive by sharks!"

At the word *sharks,* somebody burst into tears.

Mom yelled, "Ben! That's enough!"

But the water. It was everywhere. An inch at least all over the floor.

"Charles, check the bathroom," Dad said.

Okay, I'm checking. What am I looking for? I don't know what I'm doing.

"Well?" he called to me.

"I —"

"Is it wet in there?"

"Yes."

"Just the floor, or can you tell if something's leaking?"

"Just the floor. I think."

I don't know. How am I supposed to know? My job was sanding and scraping. I don't know how to fix a leaky boat.

"What's causing it?" Mom called down to Dad.

"I'm not sure," Dad hollered back. "But if I had to guess —"

He lowered his voice to a whisper: "I don't know what I'd guess."

Ben's face appeared at the top of the ladder.

"Dad? Can I —"

"Stay up there!" yelled Dad. "Everybody stay up there."

Dad covered the floor with his eyes and his feet, mumbling, "What the —? Where is it?"

Thirty seconds later, he cut the engine. Silence.

"There's no time," he said, ascending the ladder in a step and a half. Over his shoulder he yelled back at me, "Charles, help me lower the canoe in the water. Everybody else, line up on this side. We're going to put you in the canoe."

"You'll ruin my fishing lines!" yelled Ben.

"Dammit, Ben!" said Mom. "Do what Dad says!"

Ben burst into tears.

"Are we going to DIE?" he cried. "We are, aren't we? It's all my fault for making Laura change her vote."

"STOP IT!" Dad yelled. "We're not going to die. But I have to fix this thing. And I can't fix it if I'm worrying about you all. Now, Ben, move your fishing gear. Charles, help me with the canoe."

I helped Dad unhook the canoe — *Was I supposed to have repainted it, too?* — from the side of the *O'Migosh*. We dropped it in the water and watched it splash.

Is this really happening? A canoe? But we can't all fit, can we?

"Charles will get in the canoe first," said Dad. "He'll help the rest of you. Take your shoes off first. Everybody just stay calm. We can do this."

I threw the rope ladder overboard and climbed down backwards. I could feel my knees shaking. My whole body was clumsy with fear.

"Mr. and Mrs. Fluff!" Sally yelled, trying to lift the metal rabbit cage. "Somebody help me carry the Fluffs."

"We'll get them later," said Mom.

"I'm not going without the Fluffs!" said Sally.

"Sally, come on!" directed Mom. "We'll get them when we —"

"Where's Laura?" asked Clara.

"Where *is* Laura?" Mom yelled to Dad.

Dad looked seven hundred years old. He disappeared belowdeck.

"She's not down here," he hollered back in a voice that trembled as if even he might start crying.

All this crying isn't helping! Stop crying, everybody!

"Laura must've fallen overboard!" yelled Ben. "She'll get ate *first* by sharks!"

"Frank!" Mom cried. "I can't take this anymore! DO something!"

Dad was now back on deck.

"What can I —"

Just then a head popped up from the water below.

"Laura!" yelled Mom.

She slipped again beneath the water.

"What the hell?" said Dad, taking off his shoes and jumping in the water after her.

Then they were both gone for another half minute. Mom was crying huge raindrop tears, like Ben.

Laura and Dad returned to the water's surface.

"Okay, that's good," Dad was saying. "Now come sit over here. Charles will help you get settled in the canoe. Just wait for the others."

Dad crawled back up the rope ladder.

"She was trying to patch the boat," Dad said. "With her gum."

What?

"It's not a bad idea," Dad continued. His eyes were still wet, but now he was trying to swallow a laugh. "Patching the boat with gum. Not bad at all."

People! This is not a joke! This was how people died! We're taking on water. And we're discussing gum? GUM?

"Okay, Charles," Dad yelled from the deck. "Come with me."

"What?"

I was helping everyone get settled in the canoe. And now Dad wanted me to come back on the boat?

"I need some help," Dad said.

No, I thought. *NO! I can't!*

"Charles, let's go!"

And so I wobbily climbed the rope ladder back onto the boat and followed Dad down below, as if I were crawling into my own grave.

25.

We sloshed through the water. It was now several inches deep. This was more than a leak.

Always stay with a sinking boat.

No.

D*on't stay with a sinking boat. **Understand your swimming limitations and stay within them. 'Member you can drown in just one inch of water.**

Especially if you're a Harrisong. A Harrisong would drown *inside* a boat.

I had no idea what I was supposed to be doing. I was pretty sure Dad didn't, either. He was crawling on his hands and knees, trying to see something in a tiny space under the cockpit. Now he was using a wrench to tighten something.

"Charles, get the ragbag and start tearing clothes into strips."

"The *what?* Where is —"

"I don't know where it is! Find it!"

Oh, God. Where is it? In the galley?

"I think I saw it under the sink."

Okay! I'm looking. Past the stove. To the sink. Bend down. Open the cupboard. Smells like fresh paint. Dishwashing liquid. Windex. Sponges. Bleach. Oh, there! In the very back. A black plastic bag filled with old clothes. Remember Mom putting that box of leaf bags on the dining room table back in Normal? How long ago was that? A year? Three years? A month? A week?

I pulled the bag out, knocking over everything in front of it. I ran back to where Dad was standing in front of the dead engine.

"Now what do I do?" I asked. He didn't answer.

"*DAD?* What do I do?"

He was poking at something near the engine.

"I need strips of material," Dad said. "Just tear the clothes into long pieces."

I opened the bag and saw a light blue blouse on top. Was it Clara's? Mom's? No — Laura's. Dancing somethings all over it. I yanked the blouse out of the bag and began pulling at it hard.

It won't rip. Pull harder! Oh, God. Pulling harder. It's not ripping.

"I can't tear this!"

"Then get some scissors and cut it," Dad yelled. "Hurry!"

Scissors. Scissors. Scissors. Where are the stupid scissors? Mom's sewing box. Where is it? Where IS it? Oh. In the closet. Top shelf: pillows, blankets, sheets. Middle shelf: There it is. Get out of the way, flashlights! Pull the sewing box down. Dump it out. Where are the scissors? Thread. Thread. Thread. Thimble. Penny. Button. Charm. Pen. Comb. With thread wrapped all around it! Who put their STUPID COMB IN HERE? Where are the damn scissors? Mom's class ring from Catholic school in Springfield. Red stone. What's it called? Garnet. I.H.S. in center. "In This Sign." Somebody famous said that going into battle. Who? WHO CARES WHO? Remember how I used to think I.H.S. stood for "Illinois High School"? Stop thinking, you dope! Look look look. Feels like I'm moving underwater. I AM underwater. We're drowning, you stupid idiot. Keep looking. Black plastic cape. Ben and his damn action figures! Oh, wait, there! Scissors! Okay!

I ran back to where Dad was working. I stood there, holding the scissors in one hand, the blouse in the other.

"I need a lot of them," Dad said. His hands were covered in a gold and shiny glop. "Now!"

All right already! I'm just thinking: How do scissors work again? Is there an ON/OFF switch? Wait, this is easy. Kid stuff. Scissors are for third graders. I know how to do this.

I began cutting the blouse in jagged-edged strips. I passed them to Dad. He slathered the rags in the thick goop. What was it? Grease? Oil?

"More!" Dad said. His hairy face looked wild and misshapen, like a gargoyle's.

I kept cutting. Passing. Cutting. Passing. The blouse done. Pull out something else. A pair of Ben's jeans? Too hard to cut. Oh. That stupid neckerchief dress Mom wore to school that day. Easy. One cut. Two. Three.

Dad was mumbling something. Crawling back under. Where's he going? That's a pipe wrench, I think. Now he's opening something.

WHOOOOOOOOOOOOOSH!

A wave of water flooded in. Like a pipe had burst.

Not a pipe, you moron! That's the Gulf of Mexico.

Whatever he'd done, Dad'd made it worse. Oh, God! We were going to drown down here. And the others would escape in the canoe. Maybe someone would see them and rescue them. But we'd die down here. Dad and I would die.

The water was pouring in, faster, faster, faster.

"C'mon, Charles," Dad was saying. "It doesn't have to be neat."

Now he was using a long, thin screwdriver to pull out layers of frayed rope.

Suddenly my eyes were overflowing.

I can't see! I can't breathe! I can't swim!

"Keep cutting!"

He was grabbing the rags from me as fast as I could cut them. He was covering them with the glistening chickeny gravy sauce. He looked like a crazy man. No. Like a murderer.

You're going to kill me, aren't you? Just like in the Bible. The father with the two sons. Just like in The Yearling. *They had to kill that stupid deer. Otherwise, the family would've died of starvation. Everything will be better without me, won't it? Because then it'd be easier. With one less. Twenty percent off! And then you could see the movies you want to see and not always be so embarrassed of me. But it doesn't count unless you kill your chosen son. I'm older, but Ben's your favorite. YOU HAVE TO KILL HIM. NOT ME. But you're too much of a COWARD to kill Ben. You couldn't even kill those kids who wrote that stuff on Clara's posters. I thought you were going to find them and KILL THEM. Instead, you went out and bought chicken. CHICKEN? And cole slaw and rolls and mashed potatoes! I wanted you to KILL THEM for what they did to Clara. SMOTE THEM OUT. Turn them into LEPERS or PILLARS OF SALT. But instead you bought chicken. What kind of FATHER ARE YOU? You Can't Even Protect Your Own Children. Can't or WON'T? Because that's even worse. I hate you I hate you I hate you. If you make one move toward me, I WILL KILL YOU with these scissors. Do you hear me? I will drive these scissors into your leg so fast and so hard. I will stab you ten twenty thirty forty sixty a hundred times if I have to until you*

BLEED TO DEATH. I will! Don't think I won't. Because I'm not a coward like you are. I'm not afraid to kill somebody. If I were her dad, I would've found those stupid kids and KILLED THEM with my bare hands for what they did to her. But you just let them do it! You just stood there and let them do it. Why didn't you stop them? You're as bad as they are. Worse! Because you could've stopped it and you didn't. You just stood there LIKE AN IDIOT while they did it. They did it, but you did it, too. Because you didn't do what you could've done what you should've done and now everything everything EVERYTHING is ruined because of you and that's why I'M GOING TO KILL YOU BECAUSE SOMEBODY HAS TO PAY FOR THIS STUFF SO I'M GOING TO KILL YOU, I'M GOING TO —

Dad was saying something.

"Hold off on the rags. I think we got it."

What?

"Let's see if we got it."

He cranked the engine. He pointed to a tiny drip. Then another drip about a minute later.

"I can live with that," Dad said. "But let's wait a second to make sure."

We waited in silence, watching the drips get smaller and less frequent. Dad used a wrench to tighten the nut covering the box he'd just opened.

"Damn packing around the propeller shaft," he said. "I should've checked that before we left. We'll have to replace those rags with real packing at the next port."

"It's fixed?"

"Yep," Dad said. "I'd say so. We can start bringing the others back onboard. They must be scared to death out there. We'll get a bucket brigade going and start bailing this water out."

I couldn't think of anything to say. So I just said what I was thinking: "Oh."

And then I realized: Oh, no. I'm crying. This is bad.

"Charles?"

No, please don't.

"Come here," Dad said.

You can't help. It's too big. It's killing me.

He pulled something white from the ragbag. An old T-shirt of his. With one hand, he held the soft cloth to my face. He put the other hand behind my head and held me. "There," he said. "It's okay, Charles. We got it."

But I kept crying. Huge hot stupid tears. Gulf of Mexico tears.

"I know, I know," he said. "It was scary there for a minute, wasn't it? Especially when I pulled the old stuffing out and we took on all that water."

"Mmmm mmmm."

"You saw that old rope-looking stuff that was wrapped around the shaft? That's called the packing."

"Mmmmm."

"Charles, there's not a thing we can't fix. You know that, right?"

I was hyperventilating. He held me tighter.

"But you've got to tell me so I can help."

"Mmm mmm."

"Just tell me what it is."

"Mmmmmm."

I couldn't say it. I was blinded by my tears and dumb with shame.

"Son, let me help you."

He held me, and I whispered it into his shirt. "Sometimes I feel —"

"What?"

Uh, I couldn't breathe. I was soaking through his shirt with my tears.

"What is it, Charles?"

It's impossible to explain. How can I explain it to you?

"Like . . ."

"Like *what?* What do you feel like?"

I said it in a whisper: "Boo."

He squeezed me tight to his chest.

"Oh, Charles," he said. "I know you're blue. I know. I know. It's hard. This growing-up thing. It can make you feel so damn blue."

Blue? I said Boo. Like Radley.

"The things people do," he said.

Exactly. People like me.

I wiped my nose against my sleeve.

"I don't want to be bad," I said. "Or mean."

"*Mean?* Charles? Someone as gentle and kind as you?"

Gentle? Kind? I just thought about killing you. With a pair of scissors. I begged you to kill Ben instead of me. You have no idea who I am.

"But you know Mom and I are always here," he said. "And there's not a problem in this world that's too big to fix. Not a single problem. I mean that, Charles."

He kept holding me and talking softly.

"You'd be surprised how easy most things are to fix. Like that packing around the propeller shaft. Those rags you cut worked just fine, didn't they? We covered 'em in grease and packed them back in tight. We fixed it, didn't we?"

"Mmmm mmmmm."

"We'll need to put some real packing in there sooner or later. And we'll need to check the shaft to make sure it hasn't been scored by the bad packing. And see that coupling?

Right there? Well, that connects the engine to the shaft. Now normally what I'd do is —"

I didn't understand a word he was saying. It didn't matter. He hadn't understood what I'd said, either.

But he held me close as I stood there, sputtering, sobbing. He talked about fixing things. As he did, he wiped away my shameful tears.

Then he stopped talking and just held me tight, like he was trying to squeeze the blue — and the Boo — out of me.

26.

Dad and I helped the others back on the boat. Each one asked, "Is it fixed? Is it okay?"

"Looks like we got it," Dad said. "Common problem in old boats, especially wooden ones. Packing around the propeller shaft was leaking. Took on a lot of water when we swapped out the stuffing."

I was listening to him but thinking how strange it all was. Or rather, how strange it all wasn't. This was the flip side to the leaf project syndrome. It could make ordinary things — school-supply shopping, picking the prettiest leaves, conversations with school counselors — seem extraordinary. But it also made extraordinary things seem ordinary.

We almost died. Then we didn't. For a minute there, I thought my dad was trying to kill me. But of course he wasn't. Something huge and terrible almost happened. Then it didn't.

In any case, that was that. Back to business! It was all so unceremonious.

I heard my name mentioned.

". . . and basically that was Charles's role," Dad was saying. "Couldn't have done it without him."

What? Okay, I knew that wasn't true. Just smile. It was nice of him to say.

"Well," I said.

Well, what? What was there to say?

"You know what really helped," I said.

Where am I going with this?

"Laura's gum," I said. "I think that made the difference."

"Reeeeeeeeeeeally?" Laura said, her spine straightening like a stroked cat.

"Oh, yeah!" said Dad. "All the difference in the world. The gum was like an instant dry weld. Great idea, sweetheart."

Laura's entire body smiled.

Was Dad serious? I was kidding, but he seemed serious.

We spent the next few minutes thinking of new monikers for ABC gum: Altogether Bona-fide Crazy gum. A Beautiful Creation gum. A Bit Common gum. Also Blah (and) Cement-like gum.

"Absolutely Brilliant C-solution gum," said Mom.

We all agreed that was the best name. Laura was beside herself with happiness.

And then, as was becoming our pattern, we returned to the business of life as normal. Well, not Normal normal, but normal-for-us normal. The extraordinary ordinariness resumed.

Ben began untangling his fishing lines. I saw that he'd abandoned his eye patch at some point in the drama.

Mom said she was going to start thinking about lunch. Laura and Sally said they'd help. Dad said he needed to keep a close eye on the propeller shaft, but he'd rewire a light for Mom in the meantime.

Dad asked Clara and me to rehang the canoe on the side of the *O'Migosh*. Clara jumped in the water as I kicked off my shoes. I climbed down the rope ladder, my legs still wobbly from the day's events. (It wasn't even ten o'clock in the morning yet!)

I lowered myself slowly into the water, trying not to think about it too much, and dog-paddled over to Clara. She was treading water with grace. We tried to hang the canoe twice and dropped it, both times producing a terrific belly flop of a *SPLASH*.

Finally, on the third try, we lined up the hangers on the canoe with the matching hooks on the *O'Migosh* and counted: "One, two, three, LIFT!"

We got it.

"It's like hanging a picture," Clara said, treading effortlessly.

"A picture as heavy as a *car*," I corrected. "While you're swimming."

We were still a canoe's length apart.

"Chumsley!" she yelled over to me.

"What?" I yelled back. I'd forgotten how much I hated swimming. It felt so unnatural.

"We're synchronized swimming!"

She flipped over and floated on her back. I did the same.

Oh, yeah. Floating on your back. It's a little easier.

Clara was drifting past me. I turned my head.

"Clara?"

"Yeah!"

We were both looking up at the sky.

"Dad thinks I'm a little blue."

"A little *Boo?*" she said, still floating on her back. "You mean like *Radley?*"

She flipped over so that she was treading again.

"No way," she said. "You're more like a little Atticus. Kinda quiet, but smart, and just completely good to everyone."

I said blue. Jeez! Why is everyone in this family suddenly going deaf?

Clara was still talking.

"And definitely the guy you want on your side when it's you against the Ewells."

Why didn't anyone understand me? Or maybe everyone did.

Maybe everyone was right. I was part Boo, part blue, and part Atticus. Three people in one. A human s'more. A Peanut Buster Parfait.

Or wait. Had she heard me with Dad? Could she have heard me say Boo?

Clara swam over to the rope ladder. I paddled behind her.

"If I'm a little Atticus," I told her, "that means you're his sister. Aunt Alexandra."

We both cracked up. Aunt Alexandra! The sausage-shaped prissy aunt who comes to Maycomb to care for Scout and Jem.

"No," Clara said. "I want to be Miss Maudie. Remember? The neighbor lady who gardens all day and bakes little cakes for the kids."

Clara climbed up the rope ladder. When she reached the top, she turned around and looked at me in the water.

"Chums, you know how I know I'm right about the Atticus thing?"

"How?"

"Because remember when you were reading *To Kill a Mockingbird* to me and I made you use different voices for all the characters?"

"Yeah," I said, thinking how long ago that seemed.

"Well," Clara said, holding the rope steady for me, "you always used your own voice for Atticus."

I looked at my older sister. Her hair was pulled straight back from her forehead. Her eyes were little slits. They got that way when she was tired. But when she smiled . . . she was smiling now. God, she was pretty. She looked like a sculpture. Or a magical sea creature. A cross between a mermaid and a dolphin.

I was still treading water below.

"You're beautiful!" I yelled up at her.

Clara just laughed. So I said it again.

"I *said* you're beautiful. You. Are. Beautiful!"

"I know I'm beautiful!" she said. "Now c'mon!"

My sister, the enlightened master. Clara helped pull me up.

27.

Later that afternoon, Ben was reeling in fish. Dad was teaching Mom and me how to steer the boat.

Laura and Sally, both chewing great mouthfuls of purple gum, were making up a new song about Mr. and Mrs. Fluff in which they were the heroes who rescued the Harrisongs from death.

As daylight faded on our first full day at sea, I found Clara digging out her art supplies.

"You'll see," she said, smiling mysteriously when I asked what she was going to paint. She had filled all the little compartments in her tackle box with different-colored paints. I smelled a new mural.

Sally saw the lights first. Twinkling white lights strung between a lighthouse (*a real lighthouse!*) and a row of restaurants.

"Is that England, Dad?" Ben asked.

We were all on the deck, staring at the lights on the shore.

"No, I don't think so," said Dad.

"Isn't Paris supposed to be the City of Lights?" Clara asked. "Maybe it's Paris."

"No, it can't be Paris," said Mom. "Paris is in the middle of France. What is it, Frank? Where are we?"

"I don't know," Dad said.

"I don't, either," Mom said.

And we all just stared in silence.

"I know one thing," Dad finally said, and he clapped his hands. "Wherever it is, we're having dinner there tonight."

Dinner in a restaurant! I couldn't wait.

I remembered how embarrassed I used to be to eat with my family in restaurants; to be seen doing *anything* with my family. Then I remembered that stupid movie about the extraterrestrial dogs, and my classmates who sat in the back of the theater, laughing at the *people pooper-scoopers.*

People pooper-scoopers? I was embarrassed by *that?*

I didn't care where we were. It couldn't be Europe. (*Could it?*) No, we couldn't have crossed the entire Atlantic Ocean in one day. (*Could we have?*) It was probably just another Alabama town. Point Clear, maybe. Or Louisiana. Florida. Even Texas. (*Could we be going backwards? Of course we could!*)

Wherever it was, it looked like a dream. It looked like heaven to me. I squinted at the lights until they looked at first like Christmas tree lights and then like giant animals. Slowly they dissolved into a constellation of stars.

As we got closer to shore, we could smell food — restaurant food! — and hear a band playing on an outdoor dance floor.

Mom suggested we go around and name one thing we'd learned on our first day at sea.

Mom! You're back!

"The most important lesson," Laura began proudly, "is always pack gum."

"Always be nice to your Fluffs!" added Sally, who was holding Mr. (or was it Mrs.?) Fluff in her arms and petting him (her?).

"Never buy *anything* from a crook named Ralph Plattinbonkers," Ben said, crossing his arms.

"But Ben," said Laura, "if we *hadn't* bought anything from that man, we wouldn't have the *O'Migosh*."

"Oh, yeah," Ben said, uncrossing his arms. "Then *always* buy *all* your stuff from *Mon-seer* Plattinbonkers."

Everyone laughed, including Ben. He loved being the clown.

"I'll tell you one thing I learned," Dad said. "Mom's instincts are always right. If we hadn't left Fairhope when we did, we might've been fighting that propeller shaft battle in the middle of the night. That would've been much worse."

Did Mom look at him? I think she did. Good good good.

Clara started laughing.

"Wait!" she said. "I just thought of a really good one."

She cleared her throat, made that silly overly grand gesture with her hands, and said, "I learned that it's important to always have a positive way of thinking!"

And then she collapsed in laughter on top of Laura.

I couldn't believe Clara was laughing. About her campaign slogan! Could she have forgotten how cruel her classmates were? Could she have forgiven them?

The whole thing: the election, the posters, the hateful words, school, shopping for underwear. . . . It all seemed so long ago. So blessedly far away.

Mom needed more time to think about what she had learned on our maiden voyage aboard the S.S. *O'Migosh.*

"Well," she finally said. "I can think of two things. The first is what I learned when I thought we'd lost Laura."

"What?" Laura asked coquettishly, snuggling up to Mom.

"That the things that make me the happiest have the potential to make me the saddest," said Mom.

And I was pretty sure I knew what she meant.

"But here's the second lesson I learned," Mom continued. "I thought the perfect name for our boat was the S.S. *Seven Suitcases.* But that was before we saw it. Remember how we all stood in the boatyard that day, saying, 'Oh my gosh'?"

How could I forget? It was the day I'd thought my parents had made the most stupid mistake of their lives.

"'O'Migosh' was the perfect name for our boat," said Mom. "So I guess what I learned is that you should never pick a name for something until you really see it with your own eyes."

That, we agreed, was a good rule to live by.

"That's how we named all you kids," Dad said. "Remember how we thought Sally was going to be Isabella? One look at her and it was clear she was a Sally through and through."

"And Charles, I picked out the name Jack for you," Mom said. "But then when we saw your regal profile, we knew you had to have a more dignified name."

My regal profile? Jack? I could've been a Jack?

"Charles is turning red!" Laura sang. "He's blushing! Look!"

And everyone looked at me.

"I am not," I said, feeling my face burn. "I'm just . . . sunburned."

"Chums, you haven't told us what you learned," Clara said.

"What about it, Charles?" asked Dad.

I thought for a minute. What had I learned? Well, the obvious thing: Apparently, I mumble. And at critical times, too.

And I learned that you should always put off writing your book reports until the last minute because you never know when your parents will pull you out of school.

I took a breath before I spoke.

"What I learned is that . . . um, no matter what happens, you always learn something."

"That's a good one, honeybunch," said Mom. And she tickled my hair with her index finger, like she used to do back in Normal before I fell asleep.

When she did that, I remembered my old prayer:

God, please let us be a normal family. Let us get a normal car. Let us live in a normal house and do normal things and not always be so embarrassing and different and loud. This is all I want. Please. Thank You. Amen.

And then I remembered the prayer I'd said the last night I spent in my old bedroom in Normal: *God. Somebody. Please help me. I need a miracle. I'm begging You. Help me. Please. Thank You. Amen.*

"There's something else I learned," I said, fumbling for the right words. "Some wishes come true. Some wishes don't. Sometimes you find out you were wishing for the completely wrong thing."

This isn't coming out right. These words are all wrong, too small.

I tried again.

"And sometimes," I said. I coughed shallowly.

I don't want to sound like an idiot. Or a puppet.

"Sometimes," I said quickly, sounding like an idiot puppet.

Only Dummies Drown.

But you're not dumb. And you didn't drown. Besides, you're eleven years old. Give yourself a break. Keep trying.

"You can be rich in ways that are better than just having a lot of money," I said.

Why is this so hard to say? Just say it. Say it now because if you don't, it will get harder to say as you get older. Look at them.

"And sometimes," I continued, "even a moldy old boat can be a home if you're with the people you . . . they . . . er, love . . . or whatever. (*Ack!*) It's like . . . just all of us together . . ."

And here's the part I still can't believe. Though I didn't exactly sing it, I sort of spoke-sang: "Woo hoo, woo hoo, it's all for YOU."

That idiotic Bargain Bonanza jingle!

But instead of cringing (as any normal person would do), I smiled. A big, dopey smile. And then I started laughing. And everyone laughed. And before I knew it, Sally had plopped one of the Fluffs in my arms. (*Oh, for God's sake!*)

But there I was, petting a freakin' rabbit and laughing. Out of the corner of my eye I saw Mom take Dad's hand and squeeze it tight. I knew that was a good sign (*Hey, did I fix something?*) because now Mom was smiling not just with her mouth, but with her eyes again. She looked pretty even though I knew she'd been crying.

And Clara *was* beautiful! They were *all* beautiful. And I was, well, if not exactly beautiful (*small steps, people!*), I was okay. I was pretty okay.

It felt giddy to think this. It felt even giddier to feel the two thoughts that were floating in my mind, swirling together like the white foam and blue-black water below: *Finally, I'm a grown-up! Finally, I'm a child.*

28.

So maybe we weren't normal. We were Harrisongs! (*Welcome to Peculiar!*) And we were going to eat dinner together in a restaurant.

Maybe after dinner we would stay on land. Mom and Dad could get jobs. We'd find a new school where mean, stupid kids were banned.

To see your new school and meet your wonderful new friends, turn to page 258.

We'd buy a house.

To take a tour of your new (air-conditioned!) house, turn to page 260.

Or, we'd return to the boat and go to the next port. Or the next port after that. We'd start our new lives there. Or anywhere.

To discover a hidden island, turn to page 261.

Or, we'd live on the boat forever — on water or land.

To see your new life, turn to page 262.

But no matter what we did or where we went, it would turn out okay. Pick a leaf, any leaf. They're all pretty.

To finally grow up, go to pages 285–325.
To fall in love (if you dare!), turn to pages 294–357, 364–398, and 447–462.
To publish your first book, proceed to page 368.

Pick a leaf, a love, a life.

Pick one. Pick ten. Pick TWENTY THOUSAND MILLION!

Pick Clara Harrisong for 7th-Grade President!

Pick Atticus for God. Pick Jesus and Karenna. Pick a Pizza Hut church and the Dairy Queen.

Pick birds that can make a dress. Pick a rabbit magician pulling a rabbit magician pulling a rabbit magician pulling a rabbit magician . . .

Pick a one-syllable, one-note song about a rabbit. A bunny song. A hare's song. A Harrisong.

Think of anyone or anything you love. Then pick a door, any door. Pick a room, any room. They all lead to the same treasure.

They do?

Of course they do. It's all the same house. In my Father's house are many rooms.

(*In my sister's house, too.*)

There's only one house.

Is it haunted?

Only if you think it is. Don't worry. It's weird good, not weird bad. You'll be okay.

There are lots of books in the library. You can pick a different book.

Pick a different ending. Just turn the page.

And cross your fingers the deaf girl is working!

Wait.

What if she wasn't deaf, but kind? What if that girl at Dairy Queen heard what you ordered, but saw two scruffy little kids who, for God's sake, deserved to get a Peanut Buster Parfait once in their lives?

Oh.

'Migosh! Don't worry. This isn't THE END. You'll find more wonderful adventures in the NEXT Abracadabra U-Decide Mystery!

*　*　*

Maybe it was crazy to think it could all work out. To believe that things and people could be fixed so easily. To imagine we could really start over.

Maybe it was foolish to hope.

Did it really matter? Not to me. Not then. Standing on the deck, looking toward the twinkling lights on shore, I believed it all. I felt the night wind blow my shirt away from my body. I lifted my arms from my sides and held them out straight, feeling myself washed by the air.

The breeze was warm and gentle like the wind that blows against a child's face on a night in late August when summer still has a chance to hold off the fall.

And for the first time in my life, I felt light. In that moment of absolute clarity, I believed in miracles. Like Clara, I believed everything was possible. Anything could happen.

Because we had been delivered from Normal. *Amen. Alleluia. Abracadabra and Woo Hoo.*

Even now, years later, I still pick that night to remember (!). And when I remember it, I can breathe; I can swim. I can fly.

I pick a happy ending.